THE HIDDEN HANDICAP

HOW TO HELP CHILDREN WHO SUFFER FROM
DYSLEXIA, HYPERACTIVITY AND LEARNING DIFFICULTIES

Dr Gordon Serfontein

DEDICATION

This book is dedicated to my wife Barbara, who has helped me to understand so much of the features of Attention Deficit Disorder, and to my children Sebastian, Susanne, Dorian, Christian and Arabella, who have taught me a great deal about it.

ACKNOWLEDGEMENTS

I would like to thank the following individuals:

Doreen Murray for assisting me by putting together the practical measures which are at the end of this book.

Professor M P Keet of the University of Stellenbosch, South Africa, who stimulated my interest and love for paediatrics.

Professor Marcel Kinsbourne and Dr Tom Humphries of the Hospital for Sick Children, Toronto, Canada, for guiding me through the field of developmental medicine and learning disabilities, as well as making it fascinating.

Roger Roberts whose illustrations serve to underline the fact that the chances of a successful outcome are enhanced when all concerned retain a good sense of humour.

Rose Berger who, without complaint, typed several drafts of the manuscript.

THE HIDDEN HANDICAP

HOW TO HELP CHILDREN WHO SUFFER FROM
DYSLEXIA, HYPERACTIVITY AND LEARNING DIFFICULTIES

Dr Gordon Serfontein

SIMON & SCHUSTER
AUSTRALIA

THE HIDDEN HANDICAP
First published in Australasia in 1990 by
Simon & Schuster Australia
20 Barcoo St, East Roseville NSW 2069

Reprinted 1990 (twice), 1991

A Paramount Communications Company
Sydney   New York   London   Toronto   Tokyo   Singapore

National Library of Australia
Cataloguing in Publication data

Serfontein, Gordon.
    The hidden handicap : the connection between
dyslexia and hyperactivity in children.

    Includes index.
    ISBN 0 7318 0157 1.

    1. Behaviour disorders in children.
    2. Developmentally disabled children.   3. Learning
    disabled children.   4. Dyslexic children.
    5. Hyperactive children.   6. Attention deficit
    disorders.   I. Title.

362.4

Designed by Jane Tenney

Illustrations by Roger Roberts

Typeset in Hong Kong by Bothwin Promotion Limited
Printed in Australia by Macarthur Press

FOREWORD

My interest in learning disabilities comes from my professional position but has been made much more acute through painful personal experience.

As a parent, when our newborn first arrives, we don't realise that each carries with them a 1:10 chance of some significant specific weakness in learning. Their problems may affect areas such as spelling, reading, writing, memory, organisation, mathematics, concentration, language. To make matters worse, these problems are usually associated with some pretty difficult behaviours.

Despite apparent educational awareness, many of today's children are struggling through school with problems that cause pain, yet still pass unrecognised. It is an unfair world that makes one child have to work twice as hard to experience half the success of his mates. To make matters worse the child's only reward may be being branded lazy, unmotivated, anti-social or a behaviour problem.

Life for parents is no easier. We start off confused as to what is going on with our much loved child and before long become bombarded by an avalanche of splinter therapies. Soon we are into diets, allergies, vitamins, tinted lenses, eye exercises, motor programmes, then tutoring and more tutoring. These may help one small part of the problem, but alone they are an incomplete answer. What's more, they tend to focus all attention on the child's weaknesses and failures. As adults we survive by hiding our vulnerabilities and promoting our talents. Our children have the same needs and must be able to savour success, in something, if they are to remain happy and emotionally strong.

I find the subject of learning disabilities most complex as success at school is so entwined with behaviour, motivation, happiness, esteem and parental push. Parents are already sufficiently confused and need a broad overview which looks at the whole child and how this whole child rattles their entire family. Dr Serfontein has come up with a brilliant book which I believe to be more useful than anything previously published on this subject.

I have known Gordon for the last 10 years and continue to be impressed by his great knowledge of the subject, and his ability to understand and help families. As parents we see our children described with uncanny accuracy and are left in no doubt that the author is an understanding and supportive ally.

Finally, I wonder how many parents are just about to discover the secret of their own school failure. For us, school may have been a time of uncomfortable under-achievement, but with the help of this author, let's ensure that our children don't have to suffer the same.

Doctor Christopher Green,
Child Care Author and Head of the
Child Development Unit,
The Children's Hospital,
Camperdown, Sydney.

CONTENTS

INTRODUCTION

It is generally accepted that parents are concerned about the development of their children and nurture them so that they reach adulthood equipped to cope with the uncertainties of life. It is just as widely accepted that children who are disadvantaged in some way which prevents them from reaching equal status with their peer groups as they enter adulthood, receive not only sympathy from all of us but also concrete assistance in the form of rehabilitation centres etc. In other words, children who have visible handicaps such as blindness, deafness, cerebral palsy or intellectual handicap, evoke a communal pain in all of us which we seek to alleviate by providing suitable facilities to enable them to cope with society and learn to live a full life.

The child with a learning disability presents to the casual observer with no obvious difficulties or disadvantages. He or she has a normal physique, is able to take part in games with other children in the neighbourhood and has no problems with speech, sight or hearing. The majority of us would, therefore, accept that they have no real handicap and are not in need of any special assistance. These children have what is known as a "hidden handicap".

Although the word "handicap" unfortunately has some depreciatory connotations, its use cannot be avoided. If by handicap we mean a restriction of a child's abilities to develop appropriately, then the child with learning disabilities or with developmental behavioural disorders is just as handicapped as a child with problems in any other area of development.

As a parent of children with this hidden handicap, I am quite aware of the rejection by some sections of the community, but especially by some educational and medical professionals, of the concept of a developmental disability in learning or behaviour. For most of these people, these are not handicapped but rather normal children who are not being appropriately taught, managed or disciplined. It is unfortunate that the very people who should be assisting children with this difficulty are among those in the forefront of opposition to the acceptance of such a condition.

This book is written to share my own experiences, both as a parent and also as a physician who deals with children with this form of developmental disability, with other parents who have experienced similar difficulties. I also hope that these thoughts will reach a wider audience among educationalists and medical people, to help them gain a better understanding of a condition that affects a large proportion of our children.

Developmental disabilities in learning and behaviour are not widely accepted for political and economic reasons. Should the prevalence of this condition be acknowledged by governments or other authorities, it would then be incumbent upon those authorities to provide the necessary financial assistance for these children. Although that would involve enormous sums of money, in a developed country such as Australia, it is beyond comprehension that we are unable to afford proper programs and facilities to enable children with these disabilities to grow up to be significant contributors to society as a whole. By providing support programs there would be the added benefit of a reduction in the cost of crime prevention, as a large proportion of these children with difficulties develop into juvenile delinquents and young criminal offenders.

As this book aims to reach a broad-based audience of parents, the medical profession and other interested groups, detailed information is presented in a straightforward style.

To all the parents, relatives, friends, teachers and doctors who deal with children with developmental learning and behavioural disorders: I hope that this book gives you a better insight into the difficulties which these children encounter throughout a major proportion of their lives. I hope that it enables you to be better placed to support them, for if they cannot gain support from their immediate family or advisers, to whom can they look?

Apologies and explanations for certain terms used in the book are necessary regarding the male gender when referring to children with this condition and the female gender when referring to most professionals dealing with children who have developmental disabilities in learning or behaviour. This is not from any discriminatory point of view, but it is much easier to use one gender when referring to the people involved. It is an established fact that children with these sorts of difficulties are mainly boys and that the educational therapists, remedial teachers, etc., who deal with these children are mostly female. I ask you to accept my abbreviations upon these grounds.

CHAPTER 1

WHAT'S IN A NAME?

Parents of children who are about to enter school have two questions uppermost in their minds: "Is this the correct school for my child?" and "Is my child ready for school?" The answers are significant in helping to determine the child's future in primary and secondary education.

From his first day in kindergarten, the young child encounters new social and environmental situations with which he has to cope successfully. He has to learn to sit still in a group with ten, twenty or thirty other children, as well as be able to occupy himself for periods of time without any assistance from the teacher. He has to learn to interact with other children and with the teacher, using the cultural and social tools that he has learnt at home. Separation from the family presents a major hurdle for many children, some taking longer than others to overcome this. Throughout his education he will encounter different values and be exposed to different perceptions. He will learn to develop a relationship with each successive teacher as well as with the children around him.

Most children are able to cope with the new environment that is presented and successfully integrate into school. Others, because of cultural differences or personality problems, have difficulty settling in. This may be temporary and be resolved later or else become worse as the child moves through each class. Problems at home, such as illness or death, or separation of the parents, further complicate the child's ability to integrate into the school system.

In some instances, the child will be the victim of inappropriate or deficient teaching with which he has to cope or else start to fall behind. Most children progress satisfactorily through primary school. However, some children suffer significant difficulties and are unable to make headway at school for any one or more of these environmental reasons.

When entering kindergarten, it is assumed that the child is at an appropriate stage in his neurological development where he is ready to utilise his cognitive (or learning) skills. In primary school, the child should be moving towards developing a proficiency in reading, spelling, writing, mathematics and speech. To achieve all these aims, his neurological system must be sufficiently mature to enable him to learn in the correct fashion.

Unfortunately, many children, especially boys, do not mature at the appropriate rate in early childhood and are therefore not ready for school at the usual age. These children experience some developmental delays or immaturity in the cognitive (or learning) regions of the brain which prevent them from adequately acquiring basic skills. These developmental immaturities are usually familial and may be traced in other members of the family.

It is apparent, therefore, that children who experience difficulties in learning or developing appropriate behaviour at school, may have two major reasons for their problems. Firstly, environmental difficulties may lead to distorted learning or behaviour and, secondly, developmental immaturity of the learning areas of the brain certainly place them at a disadvantage. It is convenient to separate children suffering from learning and behavioural difficulties into two groups according to the origin of their particular problem: environmental or developmental immaturity. Naturally there will be a certain amount of overlap between the two groups but the management of the condition is different for each group.

The environmental group of disabilities should be managed with the help of a developmental psychologist or psychiatrist, or possibly even an educational psychologist. On the other hand, children with developmental immaturities should be approached from an organic point of view which includes the physician, remedial teacher, speech therapist, physiotherapist and even dietitian.

This book deals mainly with developmental disabilities in children.

The modern medical term for developmental disorders of learning and behaviour is "Attention Deficit Disorder" (ADD) and has been in use for the last ten years. The educational term for developmental disorders is "Specific Learning Disabilities" (SLD). This term is used to incorporate all the various learning problems that children may develop, such as dyslexia, dyscalculia, dysgraphia and dysphasia. The term SLD was chosen as it was felt that it was less emotive and negative in the mind of the general public. However, people also tend to use the term Developmental Dyslexia when meaning SLD.

The term ADD is an unfortunate one as it describes a medical disorder purely by one of the single symptoms (albeit one of the most significant symptoms). The condition is also sub-classified into two groups: those with overactivity or those without overactivity.

It is not widely known that this condition is a very common disorder and the incidence ratings vary from 5 per cent to 20 per cent of all boys. It is mainly a male condition — approximately 90 per cent of all children with this problem are boys. Therefore, among boys, it would be one of the more common, if not most common, medical problems.

The perception of ADD as a modern condition occurring only in the last century is an erroneous one. Although the research into developmental learning and behavioural disorders has been most marked in the last fifty years or so, interest in man's capacity to learn and what determines his behaviour dates back to the early classical Grecian times. There is a direct link between the statement of Hippocrates that, "The brain is the seat of man's intelligence and the heart the seat of his soul," to our modern understanding of the brain which is still the seat of intelligence but, of course, has various other functions as well.

Towards the end of the nineteenth century, there was great interest in the function of the brain by the neurologists and neurosurgeons of that time. They studied people who had suffered strokes and, as a result, had lost functions of communication such as speech, writing and comprehension. These losses of functions were then related to abnormalities in various parts of the brain, providing us with some insight into the workings of this complex organ.

Early this century, an English paediatrician described a group of children with learning difficulties in which he supposed that the learning problems were due to some derangement of the mental processes in the brain. Later, in the 1940s, two physicians, Dr Strauss and Dr Lehtinen, described a group of children with learning problems and behavioural disorders in which it was thought that these children had some mild dysfunction of the brain.

In the 1960s, the term "Minimal Brain Dysfunction" was

coined to describe those children who had developmental difficulties in learning, behaviour, coordination or speech. The implication was that an inherent developmental dysfunction in neurochemistry affected particular parts of the brain responsible for these functions. Minimal Brain Dysfunction then became the accepted terminology for children with developmental difficulties in learning and behaviour.

In the 1970s, it was discovered that children with Minimal Brain Dysfunction did, in fact, have dysfunctions of various neurochemicals in the cognitive (or learning) regions of the brain. This will be dealt with in a later chapter but, briefly, it was found that children with this sort of difficulty had a developmental deficiency in the chemical transmitter substances that were necessary to relay messages between cells in the various parts of the brain.

More recently still, the name was changed to ADD, primarily because most parents of children with such a difficulty incorrectly assumed that the term Minimal Brain Dysfunction implied that these children had some degree of damage to their brain cells. Whatever we call it, the condition remains the same — a rose is still a rose.

KEY POINTS
- Children starting school encounter many new social and behavioural challenges.
- When commencing school, children need to be neuro-developmentally appropriate for their age.
- Learning disorders have two basic origins:
  1. Environmental constraints 2. Developmental immaturity
- Developmental learning disorders are caused by Attention Deficit Disorder (ADD), previously known as Minimal Brain Dysfunction.

18

CHAPTER 2

WHAT CHILD IS THIS?

This chapter describes briefly the characteristics of children suffering from Attention Deficit Disorder (ADD). Each aspect is discussed in greater detail in later chapters.

Basically, there are two main sub-groups in this condition. One sub-group of children with ADD displays most of the symptoms — including the problems relating to attention and short-term memory — as well as the behavioural features of activity, impulsiveness, low frustration threshold and inflexibility. Another sub-group seems to display only difficulties with attention, short-term memory or even possibly with perception. This second group of children seems to have few behavioural problems, and generally they fit in with the rest of the childhood population. They are, however, distinguishable by their lack of progress due to their learning disabilities relating to their Attention Deficit Disorder.

ATTENTION SPAN
Obviously, children with ADD experience difficulty in paying attention for a reasonable period of time. In other words these children have difficulty in focusing and sustaining their attention long enough to initiate and complete any set task. They tend to be easily distracted from the task at hand by other stimuli, such as noise or movement. Significant disturbances in concentration may lead to daydreaming and "switching off", the child often appearing to be in a world of his own. "Astral thinker" is a popular nickname as these children appear to be "off the planet".

ACTIVITY LEVEL

Many, if not most, of these children have an increased activity level compared to their peer group. They are often restless, fidgety and have difficulty in sitting still for a period of time. Of course, those who have an exaggerated form of this symptom are the ones who are classified as being overactive or hyperactive.

IMPULSIVENESS

A large number of these children, particularly those with the overactivity characteristic, tend to be impetuous or impulsive. Often they do not stop to think about the consequences of their actions and charge ahead, never giving a second's thought to whatever they are doing. As a result, they land in difficulties both behaviourally and academically. In addition, they are disorganised, haphazard thinkers and poor planners of daily activities. Their impulsiveness frequently leads to behavioural problems such as lying and stealing, or even misdemeanours such as fire lighting.

COORDINATION

One of the former terms for this condition was "the clumsy child" syndrome because so many exhibit significant problems in coordination. This mainly involves the fine motor skills which frustrate these children in learning such fiddly tasks such as tying laces or doing up buttons and then, later on, developing decent handwriting. Problems in the gross motor area also occur and delay ability to achieve that first symbol of independence — riding a bicycle. They also have problems with hopping, skipping or jumping, and skills such as kicking or catching balls are poorly developed.

SHORT-TERM MEMORY

From a learning point of view, the diminished short-term memory appears to be the greatest disadvantage. This is the ability to retain newly learned information for a period of hours, days or weeks. Long-term memory is retention of information over months or years. All new learning has to be held for a period of time so that when you are exposed to that information again, the earlier information is then reinforced and eventually consigned to long-term memory. Children with ADD have special difficulty with retention of auditory (or verbal) information. Consequently when they learn something new and are re-exposed to it a week or two later, they are unable either to reinforce the previous learning or to recall it.

INFLEXIBILITY

A large number of children with ADD appear to have an inflexible personality. They are frequently dogmatic in their attitudes and resist any change to their environment or routine. Performance within a set routine is easier and their reluctance to accept change leads to temperamental out-bursts and mood swings. Their threshold for dealing with frustration also appears to be lowered, exaggerating their inflexible nature.

OTHER EMOTIONAL TRAITS

Children suffering from overactivity are particularly liable to certain aggressive tendencies and, generally speaking, are more likely to perceive threats in their immediate environment than do other children. They react to these threats by withdrawing or by attempting to dominate, often with some aggression. Their development of self-esteem is constrained, leading to problems with self-confidence. Many display a certain superficiality of emotion and fail to learn from past experiences. They are therefore less confident when mixing with their peer group. If severe enough this lack of confidence leads to feelings of paranoia.

SLEEP PATTERN

Previously it was assumed that children who are hyperactive would have some disturbances of sleep. This is not entirely true and many hyperactive children sleep very soundly. Either way, they exhibit certain interesting features. Those who sleep soundly frequently are people who talk a lot in their sleep or are prone to night terrors or even walking in their sleep. Others have difficulty in falling asleep or wake frequently during the night. Many are very early risers and are up at about 5 or 6 o'clock in the morning.

APPETITE

Disturbances in appetite are frequent in children with ADD. Those children with overactivity often have a much increased appetite or thirst because they need to supplement the enormous energy that they utilise during the day. Others are small or fussy eaters, usually displaying distinct preferences for a particular texture of food. In my experience the majority of children with ADD have some form of appetite disturbance in early childhood.

SPEECH

A fairly prominent feature in a large number of children with ADD is the late onset of their expressive language. These children develop speech appropriately in the first year of life but then there is a delay in the development of sentence structure and verbal expression. Many have articulation difficulties and some also have some form of stutter initially. Many of these children with speech difficulties go on to later develop language problems at school which contribute to their difficulties in acquiring spoken, read or written language.

SUMMARY

These are the major symptoms of Attention Deficit Disorder (ADD). Not all children will have all symptoms, however, all children have most of these symptoms at one stage or another as part of their developmental difficulties.

KEY POINTS
- The main features of ADD are:
  — Brief attention span — Increased activity level
  — Impulsiveness — Incoordination — Weak short-term memory — Inflexibility — Diminished self-esteem — Peer relationship problems — Sleep disturbances — Appetite changes — Speech disorders
- Not all children with ADD have all symptoms.

CHAPTER 3

WHERE DOES IT COME FROM — WHERE DOES IT GO?

If developmental difficulties are so common, what is their cause? As is usual with problems relating to children, our initial instincts are to look to the pregnancy and subsequent birth of the child to ascertain the cause. However, research has shown that there is no greater incidence of ADD in children who had prejudicial birth histories compared to children who had problem-free births.

In a well known twin study, it was found that if one twin of a non-identical pair had ADD, there was only a 19 per cent chance (slightly higher than the national average) that the other twin would also have it. However, if one twin of an identical pair had the problem, there was virtually a 100 per cent chance that the other twin was also affected.

These facts, coupled with the observations of many researchers that relatives of children with ADD also displayed various features of the condition, led to the modern acceptance that the disorder is essentially a genetic one.

It would appear that the difficulty is almost certainly inherited by the child, frequently through the male line of the family because of the male predisposition to the disorder. Females are at risk of having the condition but at a much lesser incidence than males, tending to instead be generally carriers of the genetic material.

To gain some understanding of the basic difficulty, I would like to relate the brain cell and its workings to that of a car battery. As we all know, a car battery consists of a positive and a negative electrode. These electrodes are placed in a box which contains battery fluid. A spark is conducted from the positive electrode to the negative electrode via the battery fluid which then generates electricity. However, no spark occurs if there is no battery fluid. See Figure 1.

A brain cell is very similar in structure to that of a car battery — it contains a chemical fluid within the cell. The cell has to transmit an incoming message from one end of the cell to the other end of the cell and then to pass it on to subsequent cells. This message is transmitted by means of the chemical fluid in the cell. These fluids are known as neurotransmitters, and the one that is involved in ADD is known as dopamine. These neurotransmitters are pro-

Figure 1
A Car Battery

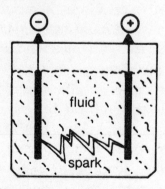

Electrical energy
is produced

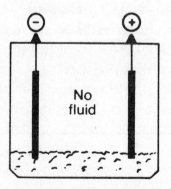

No electrical
response is produced

duced by the cells themselves.

Figure 2, on the following page, sets out the basic chemical structure of the neurotransmitter system. An incoming message will stimulate the release of the neurotransmitter substances into the space between two brain cells. This transmitter fluid then travels to the next cell where it attaches itself to the outer membrane of that cell. As a result of the attachment, the second cell then becomes stimulated and the message is passed on through that cell on to the next one. Once the neurotransmitter fluids have served their purpose, they are broken down and excreted through the body's urine.

As with all systems or societies, we have a police department here as well. In the gap between the two cells there exists a set of enzymes which act as policing agents. They control the amount of neurotransmitter fluid that is released into that space. If too much neurotransmitter is released then the enzymes destroy it to keep the level constant. This is a natural check mechanism that occurs in all instances.

In children who have ADD, there appears to be an immaturity of the cells in the affected area of the brain. Consequently, insufficient neurotransmitter is manufactured and, therefore, transfer of messages between cells is diminished. In addition, the policing system appears to be far too efficient and the enzymes destroy the neurotransmitter substances too rapidly, as soon as they are released into the space between the cells. This leads to a significant reduction in the amount of the neurotransmitter that is released into the gap between the two cells. Consequently, there is a breakdown in transmission of messages between the cells in the affected area.

Figure 2
Transmission of messages — Normally

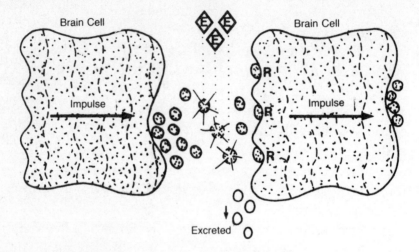

In children with ADD
(brain cells in affected area)

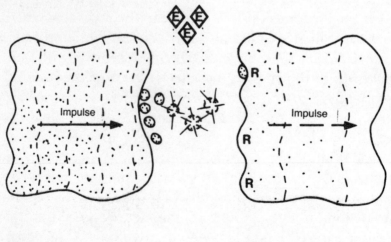

 Neurotransmitter (Cell fluid)

Inactive Neurotransmitter

Enzyme

R Receptor

Although the situation exists in the brain at birth, manifestation of these changes only occurs as the child reaches infancy. The various features become more pronounced with age, reaching a peak in the primary school years. In high school, there is a steady improvement in the symptoms, approximately from the age of 14 onwards. It appears that, at this stage, the affected area of the brain undergoes a maturation phase resulting in improved neurotransmitter release. This is often referred to as a "catch-up" stage and the children are regarded as "growing out of the condition".

However, in some people, the residual difficulties relating to attention span, impulsiveness and overactivity continue into adulthood.

The eventual outcome of the condition depends upon its management during childhood. Children who have not received any form of management or treatment invariably develop behavioural or emotional difficulties which persist well into adulthood. They frequently encounter learning difficulties which affect their career prospects.

KEY POINTS

- ADD appears to be hereditary.
- The basic problem appears to be deficient levels of neurotransmitter substances in brain cells.
- Affected brain cells appear to be immature.
- Maturation in late adolescence appears to occur in most cases.

CHAPTER 4

PAYING ATTENTION

The characteristic of diminished attention has given this condition its modern name. Invariably, children with ADD have some problem with their concentration or attention. There is a distinct difference between the qualities of attention and concentration.

Attention is an awareness that the child has for his surroundings and an alertness to the changes in that environment. This is referred to as an attention span.

Concentration is the ability of the child to focus upon one particular feature of that environment and to direct his attention and thought processes solely to that particular feature. Children with ADD frequently have problems with both attention and concentration but may only have difficulties with one.

The children with an attention span problem tend to be very easily distracted. They make themselves noticed by responding to even the slightest noise in the classroom. Restlessness or fidgetiness is often a feature of their behaviour and they frequently disrupt other children.

Children who cannot concentrate, however, are daydreamers. They are aware of various aspects in their environment but have difficulty in concentrating on a selected topic. They usually select something of more interest to themselves, such as the afternoon sporting activities or a forthcoming party, rather than what is being taught in the classroom. Typically they are the procrastinators in life and will generally put off until tomorrow what should be done today. They have problems in starting work assignments and also completing them.

Their course through school is characterised by a trail of unfinished projects left behind them. One of the most common complaints from school teachers is that these children take a long time to initiate or complete work, if it is done at all. Ten minutes of homework can often take two to three hours to be completed because of daydreaming.

A child who is not readily distracted, but is just a daydreamer, often will not be noticed in a classroom situation. Many of them sit quite still, do not draw attention to themselves and do not disrupt the class proceedings. They are quite happy to "tune out" after the lesson and entertain themselves with more interesting thought processes. On the other hand, a child with attention span difficulties is very easily and quickly detected because of his distraction and restlessness.

At home, the daydreamer will not easily respond to instructions from his parents because his thoughts are elsewhere. In the young child this can be so pronounced that the parents will think that the child could be deaf. When hearing is checked and found to be good the parents become even more perplexed. The difficulties for these children are essentially in their listening skills but many also have poor observation skills — these children will often look at something but not register what it is.

At home the readily distracted child will flit from one play activity to another and also be constantly on the move. He will be restless even when watching television and will assume all sorts of postures on the floor or on the sofa, often to the irritation of other family members present.

There is often a certain amount of selectivity in the attention deficit that afflicts these children. In fact, at one stage, the condition was called Selective ADD. A strong motivational component is involved in the ability to focus and sustain attention, and this affects these children just as much as anyone else. They are often able to sustain their attention and to focus appropriately if the subject of interest is of great importance to them. However, these selective interests are few and not widely based. Eventually, even when the subject is of intense interest to the child, attention starts to wane and repeated exposure to the subject eventually results in an attention deficit, similar to the difficulties encountered in other areas.

KEY POINTS
- Attention is an awareness of the environment and its changes.
- Concentration is the ability to focus upon one specific feature in the environment.
- ADD involves dysfunctions of both attention and concentration.
- Attention span problems result in distraction and restlessness.
- Concentration problems result in daydreaming.

CHAPTER 5

ACTIVITY — TOO MUCH OR TOO LITTLE

One of the earlier names for the condition of ADD was the Hyperactive Child Syndrome. A large number of children with ADD do have an increased activity state as one of their symptoms. However, many children with ADD have no increased activity and there are a few who have decreased motor activity (the hypoactive group).

The child with increased motor activity shows symptoms in early infancy, if not in the first year. His motor milestones are usually advanced and, once mobile, he moves around like lightning. The parents have a job keeping up with him as he darts from place to place. This speed is invariably accompanied by impulsiveness, causing him to leap before he looks. The close connection between impulsiveness and overactivity caused the condition, at one stage, to be called the hyperkinetic-impulse disorder of children.

This overactivity prevents these children from keeping their hands to themselves. They touch things constantly and are always fiddling or twiddling with something. In fact, even when they are older, careful observation will reveal some form of continuous movement involving the legs, feet, arms, hands, lips or tongue.

The very overactive child taxes the resources of his parents to the extreme and the home has to be made virtually childproof. These children are indiscriminate in their disregard for objects, be they expensive or cheap, and the parents' challenge is to remain one step ahead to prevent accidents. Visits to shops, especially supermarkets, are particularly exhausting. Gondolas with stacks of tins, etc. are a hyperactive child's garden of delights. Shopping trips often end in a state of frustration for parent and child.

Once starting school, the overactive child has difficulty in cooperating in group activities and prefers to do his own thing. Increasingly immature behaviour results in poor interaction with others, often exaggerating the overactivity.

Progress through primary school is characterised by continuing restlessness and fidgetiness and the child has little ability to sit still for any period of time. He feels compelled to get up and walk around the classroom, though not deliberately wanting to be naughty or disruptive. The need to be physically mobile is a neurological one.

ADD children who have a lesser degree of overactivity are usually just restless or fidgety. They constantly shift chairs, fiddle with rulers or pencils, or open and close school bags. A large number would be regarded as busy or boisterous people.

The hypoactive child, on the other hand, will often be missed in childhood. He is the one who is more sedentary or lethargic and is not much interested in physical activities such as sports or games. He is quite happy to sit still but, all the same, has a concentration problem. The problem here is less with attention or distraction and more with concentration. They are greater daydreamers.

Fortunately, at about the age of twelve, the overactivity improves significantly and, during adolescence, these children can often alternate between being overactive and underactive. In my experience many of the very hyperactive children, when they reach twelve, become hypoactive. In other words, they move from being flippers (flipping around) into being floppers (flopping down more often).

A number of children with ADD still have increased activity levels as adults and they often are able to direct that increased activity into more constructive pursuits.

Overactivity is also a matter of subjective observation. It depends to a large extent on the home environment as well as the demeanour of other members of the family. In a quiet family, a child who is just a little more than lively, but not out of keeping with the average for the age, would appear to be overactive to other members of the family. On the other hand, in a family where most of the members are very active, busy and lively, a child who has increased motor activity will not necessarily be noticed by the rest of the family. I have seen children, about whom the parents have been concerned regarding their learning and their concentration, but about whom the parents have not been concerned regarding their activity level, as it has not been significantly different to that of the other family members. The increased activity becomes a problem when it is causing disturbance to the rest of the family or disrupting other people in society.

KEY POINTS
- ADD children may be overactive (majority) or underactive (minority).
- Hyperactive (overactive) children are continually active with few quiet breaks during the day.
- Hypoactive (underactive) children are dawdlers who rarely get things done.
- Observation of activity levels in a child may be relative to other children in the family.

CHAPTER 6

IMPULSIVENESS — WILL I OR WON'T I?

Impulsiveness is a disabling condition for children with ADD. It is most commonly associated with overactivity, being rare in children who do not display symptoms of overactivity.

The impulsive child is most impetuous and, basically, his dictum is "act before I think". A most exaggerated example of this condition is the child who runs across the road without looking or is always jumping out of a tree thinking that he is Superman, giving absolutely no thought to the consequences of his actions. In their younger days, these children have no concept of danger and are at extreme risk to themselves and also to others. A study done by the Children's Hospital in Sydney, Australia, has found that the largest number of childhood accidents between two and ten years of age is attributable to males with impulsiveness as part of ADD.

When impulsiveness is coupled with increased motor activity, it is enough to put the parents into a psychiatric institution. In these cases, we have extreme speed and agility of hyperactivity coupled with complete lack of constraint as a result of impulsiveness. These children act upon the first thought that comes into their heads. They are the ones who stick their fingers into electric fans or put their hands on stoves or, as in one case, a child who thought it would be fun to suck tea through the spout of a teapot sustaining significant burns to the inside lining of his mouth as a result. I have known children to jump from balconies, walk on the tops of roofs or high walls, and another one who locked his mother in an aviary while he ran rampant with an electric power saw.

There are less extreme forms of impulsiveness which manifest themselves in the characteristics of disorganisation, poor planning techniques and haphazardness. These children never have the right equipment, are always late or in the wrong place, causing them to rush at the last minute in an effort to get up to date.

Scholastically, impulsiveness is also seen in examination situations. Question papers are not read with care and attention because of a desire to get started as soon as possible. Incorrect assumptions are then often made which result in inappropriate answers. This characteristic actually affects most of these children throughout their lives in that they are frequently making incorrect deductions and value judgments as a consequence of this hastiness.

In addition to impulsiveness, many children display symptoms of impatience and intolerance. Great difficulty is experienced in waiting for anything and often to such an extent that lack of immediate acquiescence on the part of the parent results in a temper outburst. Frustration of the child's desires leads to insistence, nagging and wearing down of the parent.

I have seen many children not so impulsive, but certainly very impatient, who are living examples of the proverb, "more haste, less speed".

A very good example of this is children that I see in my rooms who have to undress for examination. Included in this is removing their shoes. Impulsive children are too impatient to take the time to undo the shoelaces properly before taking their shoes off, but pull vigorously at the laces to undo them as quickly as possible, frequently knotting them in the process. When this is not successful, they then kick off their shoes as best they can, so that they can run to the scale and be weighed and measured. However, after the examination and the weighing has been completed, they have to return to their chairs and dress themselves. The undoing of the knots in the shoelaces is often of diagnostic usefulness, as they have equal impatience in trying to undo the knots and eventually hand the shoes over to their parents for undoing. Many of them become extremely frustrated in the process and tend to throw the shoes to one side, curse or swear, or even blame other members in the room for the shoelaces having been knotted.

KEY POINTS
- Impulsiveness results in "leaping before looking".
- Impulsiveness is a major cause of accidents in young boys.
- Disorganisation is often a feature of impulsiveness.
- Many impulsive children are also impatient.

CHAPTER 7

COORDINATION — WOBBLES AND FUMBLES

Coordination is largely divided into three areas: gross motor, fine motor, and eye/hand or eye/foot coordination.

Gross motor coordination is the ability of the child to coordinate his large muscle movements and perform various tasks. As a result, children learn to walk, run, jump, ride a tricycle or a bicycle, balance themselves properly on one or two legs, and to hop on one or two legs.

Fine motor coordination is the development of fine muscle movement for more exacting tasks such as placing blocks one on top of the other or playing with Lego; doing up buttons or learning to tie shoelaces and, eventually, acquiring an appropriate handwriting.

Eye/hand or eye/foot coordination skills enable the child to use his hands and feet in conjunction with his eyes. This facilitates activities such as catching, throwing or kicking balls, racquet or batting sports as well as playing a role in the development of handwriting skills.

Children with ADD, frequently, if not more commonly, have difficulty with one or more of the coordination areas. Certainly, the majority have some form of fine motor co-ordination difficulty which affects their handwriting. Poor handwriting skills are very common in the child with ADD affecting both the printing and cursive forms. It is interesting that some children with ADD cope better with printing than with cursive or the other way round. It is difficult to predict which child is going to find it more comfortable to print or to do cursive. Though writing is not necessarily meant to be a work of art, the child needs to acquire proficiency in communicating his ideas in a written form to others in a fairly speedy and legible manner.

Gross motor coordination difficulties are less common than fine motor coordination problems. Children suffering with the former are usually awkward or ungainly in walking and have difficulties in learning the usual childhood activities such as bicycle riding or skateboarding, or even running appropriately.

Eye/hand coordination difficulties can affect the child's ability to copy from the blackboard in addition to creating a handwriting problem. Children with these difficulties also have trouble with ball sports.

Clumsiness need not only be an academic difficulty for a young boy but also a social problem. Most young boys interact at their best when they are playing some form of game, either in the school playground or in the park near home. Any boy who is not able to engage in these activities with a fair degree of proficiency is often rather rudely left out of not only those activities but other social events. Coordination disabilities usually improve with occupational therapy or often with maturation. However, this does not occur before the age of 10 or 12 by which stage the child will have met with some buffeting in his social intercourse. For that reason, it is often wise for a child with coordination difficulties to receive a course of occupational therapy to improve the condition as soon as possible and in that way improve his social interaction.

It is important to note that not all children with ADD have coordination problems and some are quite skilled in their motor movements. I have observed many children with undoubted ADD who are able to construct the most elaborate, painstaking, and very neat drawings and sketches. I have also seen many who are very skilful in physical sports and games, and are able to run across a balance bar without any difficulties with balance or control.

KEY POINTS

- There are three main forms of coordination:
  1. Gross motor
  2. Fine motor
  3. Eye/foot and eye/hand
- Most ADD children have difficulties in at least one of the above.
- Physical clumsiness may also lead to social problems, especially for boys in sporting areas.

CHAPTER 8

SPEECH

It has been estimated that up to 60 per cent of children with ADD have some dysfunction of early speech development. Although these children usually acquire speech at the appropriate stage in the first year of life, they tend to be late in further extending and developing their expressive language.

Usually, children with ADD develop an appropriate receptive vocabulary in that they can understand the language of their immediate family. However, the child's ability to express himself is often delayed. The development of two and three-word sentences usually comes later, about the age of three years. I have seen many children with isolated speech delay until the age of five or six before expressive speech occurs.

It is a common misconception among parents that a child who has an isolated speech delay, has what is called a "tongue-tie". Tongue-tie refers to children who have a very short frenum, or tissue attachment, underlying the tongue. In the majority of people, this frenum is quite far back and connects the tongue to the floor of the mouth. Some children are born with this frenum quite far forward and it would appear that the frenum impedes the movement of the tongue. It is wrongly assumed by many that this causes speech difficulties.

Speech difficulties include not only the inability to develop the various sounds and articulations, but also the delay in the ability to construct appropriate sentences and the necessary syntax. These children risk having sequential difficulties both within words and within sentences. A child with this sort of speech difficulty will frequently speak of "pisghetti" instead of "spaghetti", "melonade" instead of "lemonade" or they will say, "I ball the catch" instead of "I catch the ball".

Speech is one of the highest functions of humans and, of course, is the function that separates us from other animals. Our ability to communicate in spoken form with each other sets us apart in the world of nature. Language is the use of speech to translate to others complex ideas, both in a spoken and written form. Children with ADD risk having both speech and language difficulties. Speech problems are present usually in the pre-school age-group whereas language disorders are more prevalent in the primary school age-group.

Written language dysfunctions are seen not so much in the actual writing style but in the child's ability to use written expression. Compositions are usually very concrete or literal in their expression of ideas and telegrammatic rather than descriptive.

A small proportion of speech problems manifest themselves as stuttering. This type of stuttering is the result of the child's short-term memory difficulties. As he is formulating an idea, he has problems in retaining the various units of that idea long enough to complete the whole thought and then to utter it. He often gets to the end of his thought process only to discover he has forgotten the first part, and hesitates as he tries to reformulate the idea.

In most cases, the speech difficulty can be noticeably

improved by speech therapy, but, in many cases, there is a spontaneous resolution before the child has need for speech therapy. If there is no improvement by the age of eight or nine in the speech itself, these children invariably continue to have speech difficulties into adulthood, persisting to lisp or have problems in articulating the "r" sounds or the "l's". Language disorders, if not corrected in primary school, may continue into high school and adulthood. Difficulties are experienced with tenses (usually mixing tenses), nouns, adjectives, adverbs and jumbled syntax.

There is little doubt that the child with a significant speech or language disorder risks developing a specific learning disability in either reading, writing or spelling.

There is no evidence at this stage, however, to suggest that a child with a speech or language disorder risks developing an isolated problem with mathematics. Many workers in the field attribute this to the fact that the speech area is situated in the left hemisphere of the brain, while the major input area for mathematical computations is situated in the right hemisphere.

KEY POINTS
- Many ADD children have some form of speech or language dysfunction such as:
  1. Delayed onset of speech
  2. Articulation difficulties
  3. Problems with sentence structure
  4. Disorder in sequencing of sounds
- School problems include poor written expression.

CHAPTER 9

SHORT-TERM MEMORY — IN ONE EAR AND OUT THE OTHER

The proper development of short-term memory is central to any child's acquisition of basic learning skills. Short-term memory is distinct from long-term memory in that it is the part of the memory that retains new information and holds it for a period of time, which might be days, weeks or even a couple of months. Should the child, within that period, be re-exposed to the same information, then it is reinforced and, eventually consigned to long-term memory where it will stay for anything up to a couple of years. When a child recalls information, it is taken from long-term memory and then held in short-term memory while he formulates his current idea, adding other information before that particular task is executed.

Short-term memory is obviously crucial to a child's ability to learn. If he does not retain the new units of information for a particular period of time then, when he is re-exposed to that information, the previous information has already been lost and he is not able to build upon the pre-existing knowledge — he is back to square one. This is very much like learning in invisible ink.

Short-term memory is really an extension of attention, though some people see these as two distinct entities. Once a child has attended to an incoming stimulus, he has to retain that stimulus for a period of time so that it can be reinforced by re-exposure. This is central to learning. If there is no short-term memory, there is no learning.

As children with ADD almost invariably have a short-term memory deficit, the most significant aspect of the ADD disorder, the modern name Attention Deficit Disorder is really inappropriate.

Short-term memory difficulties in ADD appear to be mainly in the auditory sector. In other words, these children have more difficulty retaining spoken information than visual information. They frequently retain visual information very well, or even at an above average level, seeming to compensate for the poor auditory short-term memory with improved visual short-term memory ability.

Characteristically, these children are given instructions and, even though they may listen to the instructions, they do not retain them long enough to fulfil them completely. They often confuse the order of instructions — an auditory sequential memory difficulty. For example, when Johnny is told to go and brush his teeth and put on his pyjamas, he is often found later in his room not knowing what to do.

It does appear, at times, as if these children are receiving information through one ear but losing it rapidly out the other. I have known children who have learnt their multiplication tables and known them extremely well only to find, half an hour later when tested, that they have not retained the new information. The newly learnt mathematics had faded very quickly. Other children have read a page of literature but upon turning to the next page, fail to recall the previous page.

In other cases, the short-term memory problem can be slightly more subtle, such as in the child who is having problems with doing additions and subtractions in columns. In this instance, difficulty is experienced in remembering which figures were carried forward to the next column or subtracted from the previous column. They, therefore, need to be helped concretely by writing down the carrying numbers at the top of the next column.

Short-term memory difficulties also affect the child in both written and verbal expression. As the child gathers the information, and is trying to collect it into a single thought sentence, the various units of the sentence are lost before the child is able to formulate the full idea. After repeatedly trying to formulate the idea, the child often gives up in frustration or produces work in a telegrammatic manner. I have referred to this problem also in the section on speech as these children, in their younger days, often stutter due to the short-term memory difficulty. Many teachers have observed that children with ADD have poorer written expression than verbal expression, mainly because the child has great difficulty in retaining information, recalling it mentally and then writing it down.

KEY POINTS
- Good short-term memory is essential for learning basic academic skills.
- Short-term memory may be seen as an extension of attention.
- Most ADD children have problems in auditory short-term memory.

CHAPTER 10

PERSONALITY DIFFICULTIES —
BLACK OR WHITE?

Certain personality traits are common features of the behaviour of children with ADD (particularly those in the overactivity group).

INFLEXIBILITY
One of the most notable of these features is the inflexible or dogmatic nature that these children display. By nature, they are hard or soft, hot or cold, black or white type people. There are no shades between the two extremes. When they have taken certain attitudes, or made certain decisions, they find it extremely difficult to alter those standpoints in the face of changing circumstances.

For example, a little boy with ADD was told by his mother that he would be attending a picnic on the following Saturday with some of his class friends. The little boy developed a sense of excitement and eagerness and looked forward to the picnic. However, on the day of the picnic, for some reason, he was not able to attend. Most children would feel disappointed but then seek other outlets for play on the day. However, the child with ADD greeted the news as if it were specifically arranged to frustrate him. He blamed his mother directly, burst into a temper tantrum and followed this with sulking.

These children appear to have lower frustration thresholds than other children and are more easily upset than others. What is often a minor event in the lives of most other people takes on significant proportions in the life of a child with ADD.

The inability to adjust to constant changes in the environment is so pronounced that many of these children have great problems in handling choice. I have seen a mother offer her child a red or a green ice-cream and the child is unable to make up his mind. After several minutes of discussion and haggling, the child eventually settles for the green ice-cream only to demand the red one when the green one is placed in his hand. At first glance this appears to be a disciplinary problem but, in the child with ADD, it is part of the child's poor ability to make a decision and to abide by it.

SELF-ESTEEM
Children with ADD also suffer to a significant degree from low self-esteem. The central part of the brain, known as the limbic system, plays an important role in the development of self-concept in the growing child. The combination of the limbic system with the higher centres of the brain allows the child to develop an awareness of himself, and the value of himself, in relation to his environment and to other children of his own age in particular. Because of the dysfunction in the central part of the brain in ADD, these children do not develop an appropriate self-concept that is found in other children.

This lack of self-esteem leads to awkwardness and they never feel quite at ease when mixing with their peers. This is particularly noticeable when peer interaction is in a group form. The child with ADD finds it easier to associate with children of his own age where he is dealing with only one or two friends.

As the child matures, and experiences more difficulties with his behaviour or his learning, he then also develops what is known as secondary self-esteem difficulties. The lack of appropriate progress in scholastic or social circles compounds the primary self-esteem difficulty and exaggerates what is already a fairly disabling condition. When the child with ADD reaches early puberty or adolescence he is already a boy who is quite significantly wounded as far as his social self-confidence is concerned. The onset of adolescence further exaggerates that fragility of the personality.

As a result of their poor self-esteem, these children employ various techniques to gain acceptance by their peer group. For this reason, they are much more easily influenced and led by other children which, in many instances, is preyed upon. Children are very quick to recognise when they are dealing with someone who is inherently weaker than themselves, and frequently exploit this weakness. The child with ADD is, in many situations, set up by his peer group because of his willingness to gain acceptance and also because of his relative naivety and impulsiveness. They are, consequently, more prone to land in trouble than are their peers.

Low self-esteem leads to feelings of inadequacy which, for many, develops into paranoia. They feel at risk in their social circle and eventually develop the feeling that people are constantly talking about them, and not in a positive manner.

DEPRESSION
Depression seems to be a fairly frequent feature of the child

with ADD in the younger years. A study done at Sydney University, Australia has shown that depression in childhood is more prevalent in the male until the age of puberty, when the incidence changes and it becomes more frequent in females. A significant proportion of the male children who suffer from depression are boys with ADD.

It is not quite certain whether this depression is due to their lack of progress, both academically and socially, or whether it is a result of the neurochemical dysfunctions. However, in the thousands of children that I have seen with ADD, I have not seen any who have experienced depression to the point where they actually seriously contemplate suicide.

SOCIAL IMMATURITY

Immaturity of behaviour is a fairly persistent feature of the boy with ADD. As we all know, boys develop at a later stage, or at a slower rate, than girls. A boy of ten, therefore, is usually behaviourally and emotionally less mature than a girl of the same age. The child with ADD is an exaggerated form of the normal boy and tends to be significantly more immature in his behaviour and social interaction. Because of this immaturity these children conduct themselves, both at home and at school, in a juvenile or infantile manner. In the classroom, they often act the class clown and seem to feel that approval is gained if they disport themselves in this immature fashion.

There is also an emotional immaturity which may appear as a shallowness of feeling. Many parents complain that the child with ADD does not seem to experience emotions as deeply as other children do and often the emotions are inappropriate. An instance of this is a child who grieved dreadfully for many months because of the loss of his next door neighbour's dog, but showed virtually no emotion when his own grandmother died the following year. It is almost as if these children repress significant emotions possibly to deal with them more successfully later.

KEY POINTS
- Personality traits include:
  1. Inflexibility
  2. Poor self-esteem
  3. Periodic depression
  4. Immature behaviour

CHAPTER 11

SLEEP AND APPETITE

One of the most consistent and persistent descriptions of the hyperactive child is that he is an insomniac. This has been so ingrained in people's perceptions of the hyperactive child that many people have refused to make the diagnosis of hyperactivity if there is no concomitant sleep disorder.

This, of course, is a fallacy. Many children with hyperactivity sleep perfectly well. They are very active during the day but by 7 o'clock at night fall quickly into a sound sleep. However, they may be early risers and wake up the next morning at 5 or 6 o'clock.

Sleep disorders, however, are fairly common in the child with ADD. There are various forms of sleep disturbance and it appears that the most common one is difficulty in falling asleep at night. Children affected in this manner resist going to bed at night. Just when the parents have packed little Matthew off to bed and feel that at last they have some time to themselves for peace and quiet, Matthew comes charging through the living room door.

Other hyperactive children have the dreadful affliction of waking frequently at night. Up and down all night, they wear Mum and Dad out with this nocturnal yoyo.

The deep sleepers have a fairly restless sleep pattern. They move and thrash in their beds and often call out, and some of them even walk in their sleep. Their sleep is obviously a very active one, not restful, and when these children wake in the morning they tend to be quite tired.

They are also the ones who are prone to developing night terrors. These occur about an hour or two after sleep has been induced. The child wakes up suddenly with a loud cry and thrashes about, his eyes often wide open. However, he is unaware of what is going on around him and, after a while, falls back fast asleep.

There is a distinctly higher incidence of bedwetting in children with ADD than in the normal population. This is very likely due to the late maturation of the frontal part of the brain which controls bladder movement. As a result, children with ADD wet their beds periodically, if not constantly, often till as late as sixteen or seventeen years of age. However, the majority improve at approximately nine or ten years of age.

In their early years, children with ADD are likely to have distinct appetite disorders or even bizarre taste sensations. Generally, the child who is overactive has an increased appetite to support the huge amount of energy that he consumes each day. These children are, therefore, fairly ravenous eaters having one meal a day which is all day. They will usually eat anything placed before them.

The child with normal or diminished activity, on the other hand, is rather a fussy eater. Not only does he eat smaller quantities of food but also has distinct taste sensations. Some do not like sloppy food and some hard brittle food. Many do not like fatty foods and others do not like meat. It varies from child to child but, generally, the overall impression is that the child has a distinct taste sensation and he will not assault that sensation under any circumstances. The result is a reluctance to eat, or lazy chewing. On no account must the child be forced to eat. A child who has no other significant medical problem will always consume sufficient food for his growth processes.

Many children with hyperactivity appear to have feeding problems in infancy and gastrointestinal disturbances such as vomiting or regurgitation, or frequent stools. These disorders usually respond to changing the infant's formula or positioning of the child during feeding. It does appear, however, at this stage that these early gastrointestinal disorders are not related to the ADD itself, but are probably either an allergic phenomenon or due to anatomical difficulty. The high incidence of allergies predisposes a child with ADD to having an allergy, in addition to his neurological disorder.

Sleep and appetite disturbances appear to be among the earliest to improve in the condition of ADD. Usually, by the age of ten or eleven, sleep disorders are settling down and the child is entering a more stable sleep pattern. Appetite disturbances often start to improve around thirteen or fourteen, accompanying the growth spurt of adolescence.

KEY POINTS
- Sleep disturbances include:
  1. Early rising
  2. Difficulty going to sleep
  3. Restless sleeping
  4. Walking or talking during sleep
  5. Night terrors
- Appetite disorders include:
  1. Overeating
  2. Picky eating
  3. Distinct or peculiar taste preferences

CHAPTER 12

LEARNING PROBLEMS

School is an area of exploration, learning and success for most young children. Lessons provided within the school environment allow the child not only to acquire knowledge but also to use it for his developing independence. Not so for the child with ADD. For the majority of them, school is a place of initial frustration, failure and eventually loss of self-confidence and self-esteem.

When a child enters primary school, the aim is to enable that child to become proficient in the five basic skills which are necessary for entering high school. These are reading, spelling, maths, writing and speech. By the end of primary school these skills should have become virtually automatic so that they may be used for the extension of further learning, increasing the child's scope and depth of knowledge. Sadly, in many schools, this is no longer the case and it appears to be an increasing feature of modern education that less attention is given to basic skills in primary school and more to discussion and development of social issues. For that reason many children who have no developmental learning problems, enter high school without proficiency in these skills through no fault of their own.

However, even in an orthodox educational environment, the child with ADD is still at risk of not acquiring these skills because of his developmental difficulties in concentration, memory, perception, coordination and speech. To better understand these learning difficulties it would be useful to have some knowledge of the workings of the area of the brain where learning takes place.

The human brain may be compared to the workings of a computer. The computer is a system that processes incoming information and then, upon request, can provide data and other valuable information. The input material is fed into the brain computer via the senses such as the eyes, ears, skin and muscle groups. Just as an ordinary computer has its own language which must be utilised to process that computer, so too the brain has its own language. An image that is seen by the eyes, or a sound that is heard by the ears, will be transformed into messages that are recognised by the neural pathways which relay these messages to the central processing unit in the brain.

Incoming information is first registered by the brain and then compared to previous information that has already been received. This is called discrimination and analysis. The brain computer wants to immediately determine whether the recently received information is similar to, or different from, previously accepted material. If the new material is similar to previous material, then it serves to reinforce what went before and to imprint that material even more strongly in the memory banks. Should the material be completely new, then it is categorised and a new file made which is then lodged in the memory bank.

The procedure is reversed when information is withdrawn. Information is recalled from the memory centre, integrated with a new set of instructions which are relayed via the neural pathways back to the peripheral organs — the voice box, hands or other muscles in the body — to convey the idea in a written or spoken form or even in body language.

In the processing, storing and recalling of information there are various steps to be followed before any new information is properly learnt. The following list is the so-called Hierarchy of Learning in which a new stimulus follows a strict pathway, ascending from the first step until the highest one is reached. When information is sent out the process is reversed, commencing at the highest step and descending until the lowest one is reached before the idea is expressed in speech, writing or body movement.

The learning hierarchy is an ordered process by which information is obtained and also produced. When a child is exposed to some information via the eyes, ears or skin, he will focus upon it using his powers of attention. The information is then retained for a short period (short-term memory) during which the new material is registered and compared to all the other stored material (perception). If, in the next few days or weeks, exactly the same material is presented to the child, it will reinforce the previous message and the information will be stored in long-term memory for later recall.

The part of the hierarchy so far employed is available in all higher order animals. The crucial bit that separates us from other animals is twofold. Humans are uniquely gifted in being able to integrate one of the sets of input (visual, auditory, sensory) with another. We are able to relate what we see with what we hear or what we feel. So, for instance, the young child that sees the word "cat" can associate it automatically with the previously learned sequence of sounds "c-a-t". Or he may associate the colour "red" with the sound "r-e-d". This process is called integration.

The other "small step for a man but a giant leap for mankind" is the ability of the brain to originate an independent thought process and execute it without any interference from instinctual forces. Conversely, we are also able to grasp abstract or conceptual ideas which do not rely upon concrete materials for their comprehension, commonly referred to as conceptualisation.

When one views the hierarchy of learning, it is obvious that an interference at any level would affect all the functions preceding it, whether in ascent or descent. For instance, if a child had impaired vision, then the information that is collected through the eyes would be distorted and so all the other levels of the processing will receive this distorted information, which will eventually be stored. When the child recalls that information it will remain distorted, resulting in the production of incorrect speech or writing to the outside world. Also, a child who has had problems with attention will not be able to focus or sustain his attention upon a certain stimulus sufficiently. As a result, that information is not completely acquired and only partially fed to the higher regions. This leads to poor storage, comprehension and integration.

The highest level of dysfunction is in the area of conceptualisation. If a child has difficulties at this level, it does not affect anything beneath it. In effect, these are children who have diminished intellectual abilities but who can acquire and store and integrate language appropriately. They are, therefore, the children with dull intellect who can acquire the basic skills of reading, writing and spelling as well as mathematics and speech, but not be able to develop those skills into richer talents.

Children with ADD primarily have difficulties at the level of attention and short-term memory. There are also many of these children who have difficulties at the perceptual level but it is very rare for them to have problems at either the integration or conceptualisation level.

The child with ADD has his greatest difficulty at the level of focusing and sustaining his attention upon the information that has been acquired at any given time. As he is not able to sustain his attention and acquire that information properly, he cannot retain it and therefore cannot perceive it appropriately.

Some children also have difficulties at the perceptual areas and, although they receive the correct information, they are not able to register, categorise or compare it with other information previously received. These children are therefore in danger of making the fundamental errors of perception that are most commonly associated with developmental dyslexia. For example, the child who constantly reads the word "was" as "saw" is very likely attending to it and retaining it appropriately but, in his actual categorisation and sequencing of that information, he is reversing it. Again, a child who is listening to the word "pat" may hear it incorrectly as "pad". The frequencies of the sounds "t" and "d" are very close, with discrimination between them being difficult. These are called auditory discrimination problems. (Examples of perceptual disorders are included in the practical procedures at the end of this book.)

The singular most serious disability in children with ADD appears to be the short-term memory problem. This is particularly so in the ability to retain verbal information. As these children are not able to retain new units of information, they are not able to build upon them and, therefore, are always risking having large gaps in their basic skills.

KEY POINTS

- Primary school should equip the child in the five basic skills:
  1. Reading
  2. Spelling
  3. Writing
  4. Maths
  5. Speech
- The brain processes learning according to the following hierarchy:
  1. Sense organs (eyes, ears, skin)
  2. Attention
  3. Short-term memory
  4. Perception
  5. Integration
  6. Long-term memory
  7. Conceptualisation
- ADD children dysfunction at levels of attention, short-term memory and perception.

CHAPTER 13

BASIC SKILLS — THE TRADITIONAL THREE R'S

The majority of children with ADD develop another form of learning disability. In many cases it is just a mild dysfunction, causing them to underachieve according to their age level. In other children the problem is more pronounced and they have distinct difficulties in acquiring basic skills.

Children with ADD risk developing specific learning disabilities or developmental dyslexia. Dyslexia is an emotive term which is used to describe those children who have difficulties with reading. In fact, the term "dyslexia" is the Greek word for "difficulties with reading". However, by this term, we refer to that group of children in whom the reading difficulties are caused by developmental dysfunctions in the learning areas of the brain. If you are a purist, then the correct terminology is dyslexia for reading problems, dysgraphia for writing problems, dysphasia for speech and language difficulties and dyscalculia for mathematical difficulties. The preferred term today is "Specific Learning Disabilities".

Children are classified as having specific learning disabilities if they fulfil three criteria, according to the International Definition. Firstly, there must be an established discrepancy between the child's intellectual potential and actual achievement in the basic skills. In other words, formalised testing must show a lack of achievement in the child according to expected levels derived from intelligence testing. Secondly, no other physical, emotional or social disability must be found to be causing the problem. For example, epilepsy, anxiety or cultural deprivation. Thirdly, a dysfunction in one of the cognitive (or learning) processes in the brain must be demonstrated. Psychological or neurological investigation must reveal a disturbance in one of the features in the learning hierarchy (see Chapter 12).

By far the majority of children with ADD suffer diminished abilities in their reading, spelling and writing skills. A smaller number have difficulties mainly with mathematics. There is a group that has difficulties with all the basic skills and are not separated into primarily language disorders or mathematical disorders.

By and large, the child with a language disorder has a problem in the development of his auditory or listening skills. Reading is mainly an auditory task — the words are being silently sounded out for analysis in the brain. The child with reading difficulties experiences problems in concentrating on the spoken word, then problems in retaining it and eventually perceiving and analysing that word.

The child with mathematical skills difficulties tends to have problems in the visual side of his learning hierarchy and the difficulties reside in visual attention, memory and perception. Children with both visual and auditory difficulties have problems in all the basic skills.

READING DIFFICULTIES (DYSLEXIA)

For proper acquisition of reading, the developing child needs two processes to be intact. Firstly, he needs to learn to sound out unknown words by breaking them up into component parts and then blending them into the whole word. This is referred to as phonics, or phonetic skills.

Secondly, he needs to develop the ability to visualise various sections of words or a whole word as such. When he hears a word, he must learn to call up the visual image of that word in his mind. In this way the child develops the ability to integrate what he hears with what he sees which allows him to automatically add words to his vocabulary. A new word that has been learnt and relearnt is eventually consigned to the child's sight vocabulary and is one that can be read instantly upon recognition. This, of course, is a necessary requirement before the child can develop spelling skills of any significance.

From the above, it is evident that all children who attend primary school should be inducted into the proper forms of both phonic skills as well as visual learning. The usual process is for the phonic skills to develop first because the auditory component of reading is so much greater than the visual component. This is the basis of the development of reading unknown words. School systems that teach only the phonics system or the visual (look and say) system in isolation of each other are erring in their teaching of the child. The development of both systems is essential for the child's proper acquisition of spelling and reading fluency.

Children with ADD, because of their poor attention and in many cases their impulsiveness, make many basic errors in reading which are not due to problems with perception, discrimination or analysis. These children, because they are inattentive, identify incorrect letters in the word as the initiating, middle or end sounds. They also pay little attention to the sequence of the letters and often get the sounds confused because they have collected them in the wrong order. At other times, they leave off the beginnings or endings of words as they rush their way through the reading. Impulsive children trip their way through reading, constantly lopping off sections of words or replacing words with other words. They invariably make mistakes with the small words and replace the article "a" with "the".

In many cases, children tend to read words from right to left or sequence their letters from right to left due to sequential difficulties. This is a natural occurrence in children until the age of about seven in girls and eight in boys. If this form of reading persists beyond these ages, then it usually indicates an underlying neurological problem such as ADD.

Initially, the child with reading difficulties has problems with sounding out and acquiring three letter words and, later, four letter words. As they move on, they have difficulties with vowel sounds and learning the rules pertaining to vowels. The rule of the silent "e" at the end of the word, changing the sound of the vowel that precedes the consonant, is one that is often not well acquired. These children, therefore, will read the word "hope" as "hop". They also have great difficulty in learning the rules pertaining to vowel digraphs — two vowels together, such as "oa" as is seen in the word "boat". Here the general rule is that the second vowel makes the first one say its name. The child, however, would have difficulty in absorbing these rules and would read "boat" invariably as "boot" or "bat" or even "bot".

There are frequent difficulties with the consonants as well, especially the difficult ones such as soft or hard "g", the soft or hard "c", and then consonant blends such as "st", "fl", and "str".

The next step in reading is syllabication — the ability to divide a long word into its different syllables and, having done that, to successfully decode the syllables and blend them together to make the word. Children with ADD have difficulties with acquiring this ability and syllabication needs to be demonstrated. One of their other difficulties is that, having successfully divided a word into its four or five component syllables, they have difficulty in retaining those independent syllables so that the blending process is hampered by the short-term memory deficit.

These are just a few examples of the types of difficulties that children with reading problems experience. At the end of this book, you will find a list of techniques to be used by parents and teachers in assisting their child with learning disabilities.

SPELLING

Spelling has similar cognitive processes to reading, with one addition which is very taxing upon the child — he has to recall a word, completely without assistance, in a concrete form and to hold that while writing the letters down.

For instance, if a child is asked to spell the word "cat", he has, first of all, to be able to mentally sound out the letters of "cat", then arrange them in the right sequence and hold them in that sequence long enough so that he can write the word down. The whole process is compounded by the fact that the final step involves fine motor coordination, as well as eye/hand coordination in getting the word out of the mind and onto the paper.

Children who have spelling difficulties have to contend with all the problems that are experienced in reading, but have the added need for good short-term memory. They also lack the concrete assistance of the word being in front of them.

The child who spells poorly will have difficulties with this whole range of problems, but some of them experience difficulties only with the final step in getting the word down onto paper. When asked to spell a word verbally they are able to do so, but in writing, they make frequent mistakes. Obviously, in these children, it is the final step which causes difficulties and they are unable to meet the demands of the transposition from brain to paper. Whether this is entirely due to their coordination difficulties or is also, in effect, due to short-term memory problems, is not quite clear. In writing the word down on paper, they would need to retain their word for a longer period than when they are pronouncing it. Therefore, there is the problem of a short-term memory deficit compounded by poor handwriting skills.

Generally children learn to read earlier than they learn to spell and read better than spell. It has been observed by most remedial teachers that it is usually easier to remediate a reading difficulty than a spelling difficulty. Severe spelling difficulties are genetic in origin and poor spellers tend to occur prominently throughout families.

Recent research by Swedish physicians has indicated that poor spelling is due to problems with attention and short-term memory. This research has pointed towards the inability of the child to retain the various components of a spelling word in logical sequence until it is transposed into the written form. This research has given further support to the notion that specific learning disabilities are largely caused by disorders of attention and memory.

WRITING

Writing skills difficulties are mostly due to problems with fine motor and eye/hand coordination common in children with ADD. For them, the difficulty lies in the inability to develop an appropriate pencil grip. They usually form a simian (or ape-like) grip, or one in which the thumb over-lies the forefinger at right angles.

In addition to the poor pencil grip development, there is also difficulty with coordinating fine motor movement, as well as the hand movement with the eye movement over the page. In many cases there is also a fine tremor in the hands which causes some degree of difficulty in holding the pencil correctly.

The sum result of these developmental difficulties is for the child to hold the pencil very tightly to gain some sort of control and also to fix the pencil to the paper to consolidate that control. Consequently, there is a limitation in the fluency of the movement of the pencil over the page and the writing becomes stilted and uneven. Their letter shapes are initially uneven in size and they have difficulty in spacing the letters one from the other. The spacing is very likely due to the eye/hand coordination and visual per-ceptual difficulties.

Many of these children find difficulty in developing a left to right progression in their handwriting and move more naturally from right to left. This may be a sequel to the cross-dominance that these children experience.

The ability to do printing or cursive writing seems to be divided fifty-fifty in children with dysgraphia. About half of them find printing easier as they appear to have more control in short bursts. Others find cursive writing easier due to the fact that, once they have started a word, there is a continuous flow and lack of interruption which helps to develop a rhythm in writing.

Writing difficulties do not just pertain to the actual writing. Many, if not most, children with ADD have difficulties with written expression. For some reason these children, who normally have quite a rich imagination and are able to express themselves verbally very well, are telegrammatic and concrete in their written expression. This may reflect an inability to formulate ideas and keep them in sequence long enough for those ideas to be transferred onto paper.

They also have difficulty in writing as such and find writing a fatiguing exercise. For this reason, all ideas are cut as short as possible so that the writing is reduced to an absolute minimum. I have found that written expression remains one of the most lasting of the developmental disabilities in the basic skills, continuing even into high school. Children, however, need to acquire a reasonable facility in written expression as it is necessary for all subjects.

Recent research has shown that children with writing difficulties are significantly improved in the majority of cases when they are placed on a course of drug therapy with Methylphenidate or Dexamphetamine. In one report, more than half the children with writing difficulties improved significantly with their handwriting from the first day that they commenced medication. A child who does not respond appropriately, as far as his handwriting is concerned, to normal modes of intervention and occupational therapy, should be considered for a course of treatment with medication as the writing skills problem can cause him major difficulties in the long term.

MATHEMATICS

Children with difficulties with mathematics are definitely in the minority among children with ADD. These children would constitute probably about 20 per cent of the learning difficulties in this group.

Apart from initial problems in developing skills in numeration, these children have difficulty in progressing with their algorisms. At first they find addition difficult, but subtraction presents a more significant problem.

Short-term memory deficit certainly interferes at the level of multiplication. This is the most consistent difficulty in mathematics and these children continue to have problems in retaining their mathematical tables well into high school. It is most frustrating for them in that they will learn a table and know it well and then, even one hour later, have not retained that newly learnt table. The only way for these children to learn their tables is to repeat them once or twice a day in a rote fashion, day in and day out for at least six months or so. In my experience, this is the only way for them to acquire mathematical tables, preferably doing it in a sing-song fashion. The sense of music and rhythm is usually intact in children with ADD and helps to secure newly learnt information.

Division presents difficulties because of the multiplication problems, and the combined difficulty of multiplication and division leads to problems with fractions.

Difficulties with mathematics rest upon the basis of an inability to grasp abstract concepts as well as short-term memory retention problems. These two factors continue to interfere and, really, the child only improves with his mathematical abilities when he either receives some form of treatment such as drug therapy, or standardised remedial maths teaching (for example the Kumon system) or when his brain eventually matures.

As with all the other basic skills, the success of treatment depends upon the child's desire to overcome his difficulty, persistence in remaining on task and also the degree of his difficulty.

KEY POINTS

- Specific learning disabled (SLD) children display discrepancy between potential and actual achievement.
- Majority SLD children have problems in reading and spelling, rather than mathematics.
- Reading requires development of phonics and sight skills.
- Writing requires good fine motor control and eye/hand coordination; as well as acquired left to right progression on paper.

CHAPTER 14

SCHOOL

Selecting a school for a child with ADD is one of the most important decisions to be made. It is important for all children but the range of schools for normal children is much wider than it is for the child with ADD.

The school for the child with ADD should meet certain essential requirements encompassing the following principles:

ONE
The school should have strictly graded classrooms. Children with ADD, because of their immaturity and maturational lag in the cognitive regions of the brain, need to be placed in classrooms where they are graded according to their ability level. The child would then be more able to compete with other children within the classroom at a reasonable rate of achievement and he can measure himself against the others for the development of his self-esteem. It is very important that he be within a group of children of similar abilities so that he can achieve some successes in comparison with them and, consequently, be stimulated to attempt tasks more readily. The importance of a graded classroom cannot be overemphasised.

Children with ADD do very poorly if they are placed in open plan classes or in parallel streamed classes or even in composite classes. These children cannot cope with the constant change in the level of work that occurs within these classes. It is also not fair to the teacher who needs to proportion a more significant amount of time to the child with ADD, which is impossible in a class where the levels of achievement vary greatly.

TWO
The school should provide a very firm structure for its daily activities. Work should be according to a strict routine and, generally, children should be in a position where they know what is expected of them and know that their work will be carefully monitored, corrected and the corrections explained. There must be order and discipline within the classrooms, corridors and playing fields.

The child with ADD, because of his disorganisation and great reliance upon routine and regularity and repetition, requires an orthodox and structured environment. In addition, his low self-esteem causes him significant problems in interacting with the other children in the playground. Because he tends to be a loner, he is frequently isolated and at risk of victimisation by other children. On the other hand, many of these children are aggressive in their relationships with their peer group and need to be well monitored and controlled so that these times of aggression, and also points of friction, can be minimised.

THREE
The teacher should be a sympathetic and warm person firmly in control of the classroom; strict but not autocratic. Children with ADD respond very well to some degree of praise and individual attention and stimulation. It is often very disarming to see how quickly they respond to a teacher who displays these qualities and their work tends to blos-

som overnight. I have seen many children who have made virtually no progress through a whole year of non-involvement with a certain teacher, only to improve greatly the next year when placed in a class where the teacher displays some form of understanding of their difficulties.

The teacher should preferably be the same one throughout the year. The child with ADD has great difficulty in adjusting to changes in the environment and routine and, for this reason, it causes great problems when there is a frequent change of teacher. There is an unfortunate situation in many schools that, because of certain arrangements, including maternity leave, there is a frequent change of teacher. I have known children who have had eight changes of teachers within one eight week term, which is, frankly, ludicrous. This rate of change of teacher would affect any child but the child with ADD more particularly.

FOUR

The school should be flexible enough to allow the child with ADD to repeat a year, preferably while in the infants or primary school. These children mature at a slower rate than other children and are, in many instances, behind their peer group in ability to grasp the five basic skills. It is my experience that many, if not most, benefit from spending an extra year either in infants school in Year 1 or 2, or even later in primary school in Year 5 or 6. The benefits of repeating a year are not only to allow them extra time in which to acquire and consolidate their basic skills, but also to afford an extra year allowing the nervous system more time in which to mature. With that situation, the child then enters high school having had an extra year in which to develop his cognitive skills and is thus able to grasp the concepts being taught at the different year levels.

Repeating the year often puts the child in a peer group with whom he feels more comfortable and his peer relationships improve as a result of this greater self-confidence.

Generally speaking, the best time to repeat is either in Year 1 or Year 2. This allows the child to mark time without any significant effect upon his self-esteem, and also allows him a lot of time to develop good relationships with other children. However, repetition must be accompanied by remedial intervention, otherwise the advantage is not utilised.

FIVE

Smaller classes are always an advantage. The child with ADD does benefit from individualised attention so the smaller the class the better. Large classes, in excess of thirty children, result in more distractions for the child and less attention being given to him. These children do much better when the class size is between ten and twenty enabling them to develop some form of relationship with the other children in the class as well as the teacher.

SIX

Remedial facilities available in the school is an additional bonus. I have already mentioned that the remedial education for children with ADD is best performed within the school environment. The ideal situation is to withdraw the child from the normal class for the one lesson or two that he requires each day to work at his deficient basic skill. He may then return to his normal class and continue with his development in the other subjects without any interruption. I can see no reason why, in developed countries, there are unsufficient schools providing remedial facilities in addition to all the other provisions mentioned above.

A large number of children with ADD are of superior or gifted intelligence and would be great contributors to our society. Assistance for them at this stage in their lives would have major benefit, not only to them, but to society in general. The price that is being paid is small compared to the investments that would be reaped in the long term. Many of these children require speech or language therapy and, in some cases, also occupational therapy. It would be excellent if these interventions could be afforded within the primary school situation as well. The whole idea of the child's remedial management is total integration within the normal stream in the classroom.

SEVEN
There should be no reluctance on the part of the school-teachers to assist in administering the medication of the children who have ADD and are taking required drug therapy. The short duration of these medications necessitates that these children have a lunchtime dosage. It would be a small thing for the teacher to assist in the dispensation of this medication which serves two purposes: firstly, it ensures that the child receives the appropriate dosage and continues to benefit from the treatment in improving his acquisition of the basic skills as well as his behaviour; secondly, it also ensures that no other child in the class receives the medication by accident.

These medications should be handled in the same fashion as the treatment for any other disorder such as diabetes, epilepsy, asthma or other long-term therapy. I have heard teachers in school argue that it is not their place to provide medications for children. This is a "head-in-the-sand" attitude, as children spend at least six hours of their waking day at school and, during that period, the school and its teachers are responsible for the child's development and general well-being. The analogy is the chronically ill child in hospital, for instance with leukemia, for whom the doctors and nurses may state they are only responsible for the medical situation and are not responsible for his education. On the basis of this argument, long-term patients in hospitals would not receive any education while they are away from school for the months necessary to receive their appropriate therapy.

EIGHT
High school should afford children with ADD a wide variety of choices. Generally speaking, most of these children seem to have better manual skills than verbal skills and are more likely to achieve in the manually orientated subjects. It is useful for them to be able to take courses in these subjects and achieve well, improving their self-esteem while they are waiting for their nervous systems to mature.

When the child with ADD enters high school, he is often confused by the frequent change of classroom and teacher and a sympathetic approach from the high school would help him adjust very quickly to the less structured situation without significant difficulty.

NINE
Examinations present particular difficulties for the child

with ADD. His lack of organisational skills, planning and ability to quickly assess what is important and not important, place him at a disadvantage in examinations. In addition, his difficulties with handwriting and his slowness in processing information frequently lead to examination results which do not reflect the child's proper abilities. Oral examinations and the availability of a scribe are useful aids to these students.

The child with ADD is better served by a school system which allows for a combination of frequent assessment of the child's classwork throughout the year and some form of examination. I do not feel that children with ADD should be spared examinations altogether, as these are good methods of preparing children for the work place and for helping them to develop problem-solving and decision-making abilities. However, a fair combination of continual assessment and examination would give the child with ADD a better chance to more appropriately reflect his true potential.

KEY POINTS
- School requirements for ADD children include:
  1. Graded and smaller classes
  2. Structured activities
  3. Sympathetic but firm teacher
  4. Flexibility
  5. Small classes
  6. Remedial facilities
  7. Monitoring of drug therapy
  8. Wide choice of subjects
  9. Examination aids for particular disabilities

CHAPTER 15

DIAGNOSIS AND DETECTION

How do you detect a child who is suffering from ADD in the early stages and how is the diagnosis effected? Certainly, the earlier this condition is picked up the better the result from appropriate management.

Fortunately, today there are early intervention centres available to which children may be referred for further assessment, should their development be causing concern. If the child has a physical or psychodevelopmental problem, he or she will receive early therapy to try and ameliorate the dysfunction. If parents suspect that the child has a developmental difficulty a medical practitioner needs to be consulted in order for the child to be referred to such a centre. Obviously, children with physical deformities will be picked up early. It is the child with a cognitive developmental problem who is likely not to be detected early.

Detection in early childhood relies upon a suspicion that the child is not developing as expected. The child who is overactive is first to be suspected because of his constant motor activity and his increasing demands upon the family's time and resources.

Later speech development would also be an early signal to the parents that all is not well with their child. Clumsiness may not be so apparent in the first few years, often only becoming apparent when the child goes to school.

Many display sleep disorders in the first year of life, having great difficulty in acquiring an appropriate sleep pattern. They may also be poor feeders and, in some instances, have projectile vomiting or poor suckling. Extreme bouts of infantile colic may be due to an allergy but also could be due to ADD. Resistance to cuddling, or a stiffness while cuddling, has been reported by many parents.

In the early infant years, alarm bells are usually set off by hyperactivity or impulsiveness or delayed speech development.

When the child reaches school age he is, for the first time, required to take part in group activities in a settled, usually seated, situation in the classroom. The overactive child is not able to conform to this situation. He disrupts the rest of the class in many cases and impulsiveness causes him to become the class clown. He talks constantly and is easily excited.

Coordination problems in the form of poor pencil grip, or inability to join in group games, is usually seen at this stage. Speech difficulties become more apparent and the problems with language also are then clear to the teacher. Social ineptness results in refusal to play with others and play is largely parallel alongside the rest of the children.

In a minority of cases the aggression which usually appears later may be seen at this age. These children have difficulties in relating to other children which is evident in frequent altercations with other members of the school.

Eventually, the child is taken to the physician and a diagnostic workup is then organised to determine whether the child has ADD.

The physician will look at the clinical history of the child to see whether it satisfies the requirements that the condition is of a fairly long-standing nature and there are no other significant emotional or social causes for the child's behaviour or learning difficulties. An examination will frequently reveal in the older child some signs of immaturity of the nervous system, usually referred to as soft neurological signs.

A psycho-educational profile is made including an intelligence test as well as an assessment of the child's achievements in the five basic skills: reading, spelling, maths, writing and speech.

An IQ test is performed for two reasons. Firstly, to establish the child's general potential and then to determine whether there is a significant discrepancy between the potential and the actual levels of achievements in the basic skills. Secondly, children with ADD characteristically have a large scatter of scores in the IQ test. An intelligence test consists of ten to eleven sub-tests which tap various aspects such as concentration, short-term memory, visual and auditory perception, comprehension, abstract reasoning and motor skills. The child with ADD usually does quite well in some tests, mediocre in others and below average in other tests. Most frequently, it is the sub-tests for short-term memory and concentration which are below average.

Another integral part of the diagnostic workup is to establish whether there is some form of dysmaturity in the child's central nervous system. Previously, electro-encephalograms (EEG's) were used to determine any abnormality in the electricity of the brain in these children. Studies have shown that approximately one-third of children with ADD have some form of abnormality on an EEG.

Later development of the EEG, and also other electrical

studies known as cortical evoked potentials, have demonstrated distinct abilities to identify children with ADD and even to categorise them.

Evoked potentials are brainwaves that are caused by presenting flashing patterns to the eyes of the child and also click noises to the ears. These waves are measured as they proceed from the eyes or ears to other designated areas of the brain. The speed and shape of the brainwaves are documented at various points. Any obstruction to the wave, such as damaged cells or deficient chemical transmission, will retard the speed or alter the shape of the waves.

The latest developments in these areas have been done at New York University as well as Harvard University in America. Two systems have been developed which have been termed Neurometrics and BEAM, respectively. These systems are able to measure the maturity in each area of the brain of a child and then to compare that maturity with what is expected for most children at that particular age. On this basis, a computerised program has been developed which then identifies children who have areas of dysfunction in the cognitive regions of the brain which would indicate abnormalities, such as ADD or Specific Learning Disabilities.

Until recently, Neurometrics and BEAM have been largely used as research tools. However, the further development of these instruments has been rapid and more sophisticated, and they are now used not only in the diagnosis and detection of learning disabilities, but also for the monitoring of cerebral blood flow during major cardiac and neurological operations in many American centres. Neurometrics has been further developed to be of great assistance in the diagnosis of psychiatric conditions such as schizophrenia, depression, and alcoholic brain damage.

Further aspects of the diagnostic workup include a speech and language assessment in those children who are suspected of having this disorder and possibly also an assessment by an occupational therapist of the child who has significant coordination problems.

After a comprehensive assessment, including clinical examination, psycho-educational investigation, neurophysiological recordings, speech and occupational therapy investigations, very few children with ADD would be overlooked. The child will, therefore, have been diagnosed and categorised as having a mild, moderate or severe form of ADD and also whether the aspect of hyperactivity forms part of the picture. At this stage, the child would then be ready to take part in a management program.

KEY POINTS
- Early detection is best.
- Look for:
  1. Overactivity
  2. Speech delay
  3. Clumsiness
  4. Sleep disorders
  5. Delay in learning colours
- Assessments include:
  1. Paediatric examination
  2. Educational evaluation
  3. Neurophysiological tests
  4. Possible speech or occupational therapeutic assessments

CHAPTER 16

METHODS OF INTERVENTION

All management programs for children with ADD aim to ensure appropriate development in learning and behaviour. The various people working with the child find that their individual efforts influence the efforts of other professionals in obtaining a composite improvement in the child's development.

The usual modes of intervention are as follows:

- Behavioural therapy
- Remedial teaching
- Speech and language therapy
- Occupational therapy
- Dietary control
- Drug therapy

BEHAVIOURAL THERAPY

The aim of behavioural therapy is to modify the child's behaviour so that he is able to move from negative experiences to positive experiences thus reinforcing good habits as opposed to the entrenching of bad habits.

As we all do not live in isolation, it is quite natural that whatever we do in our environment has a certain reaction upon us. The child who is impulsive or aggressive, or has frequent temper tantrums, has to be made aware of the consequences of these actions upon his family, school friends and teachers. He then needs to be assisted in modifying his behaviour so that, instead of the negative reactions that he receives when these antisocial character traits are displayed, he is able to gain positive reactions from others which help to accentuate the positive attributes of his own nature.

In most cases, some form of reward system is used in behavioural modification therapy. This is a positive reward system where he is actually given something for improved behaviour.

If the child has been misbehaving, then something that he enjoys or desires is withdrawn from him and there is a negative reinforcement of his inappropriate behaviour.

The success of behavioural modification therapy depends very much on both the therapist and the child. Many of the children have too brief an attention span or short-term memory to be able to retain what they are learning through the behavioural modification therapy and, certainly in many cases, the gross impulsiveness is of sufficient nature to override their instincts and they continue to repeat their misdemeanours.

The therapist is required to have a fair amount of patience as it often takes much time before significant gains are made in the behavioural program. The therapist should also be fairly objective and be able to prevent herself from becoming emotionally involved in the condition, as this could impair the effectiveness of the therapy.

REMEDIAL TEACHING — PARENTAL INVOLVEMENT

Parental involvement is essential for any child who is having significant learning problems. As with the behavioural therapist, the remedial teacher needs to be involved with the child, but not emotionally so that she can distance herself to observe the progress being made.

The aim of remedial tuition is to work with the child in such a fashion that he is able to use the strengths he possesses in order to overcome his weaknesses. For instance, if a child is fairly good with visual recognition of words and letters but weak in learning to sound out words, then the teacher will use the stronger sight skills to improve the weaker phonic skills. The added value of the one-to-one remedial situation is that the teacher is better able to focus the child's attention on the work. Problems with short-term memory, however, often prove to be intractable.

The best place for remedial teaching is in the school. Ideally, the child should be withdrawn from his normal class for the one or two periods per day that are necessary for him to receive the individual assistance in those basic skills in which he is experiencing difficulties. In other words, the child with a reading difficulty is withdrawn at some stage during the morning and is taken by the remedial teacher, with, at the most, two or three other children, to be given fairly detailed, individual remedial tuition. Teaching to a group that is larger than five is of no benefit as each child is not receiving individual attention.

The program for each child should be designed to meet his particular needs. It should also be a fairly structured program where the child has some form of routine, regularity and repetition.

If remedial tuition is not available within the school, the next best option is to obtain some privately. This should not exceed one to two hours per week and, preferably, should be done when the child is fairly fresh. Either early in the morning before the child commences school, or shortly after school finishes in the afternoon. Saturday mornings are a possibility, but many children play sport at the weekend.

SPEECH AND LANGUAGE THERAPY

As has already been mentioned, a large number of children with ADD suffer from speech deficiency or language disorder. These children encounter problems with articulation, stuttering or even language structure. Should this be pronounced, then speech therapy is essential.

Unfortunately, speech therapy within school is not readily available. It needs to be conducted outside of school for about one hour per week.

The speech therapist faces the same difficulties as the other therapists do in that the child usually has a short-term memory problem and so what is taught one week is not always retained the next week, which results in a lot of revision of previously taught information before new learning can take place.

OCCUPATIONAL THERAPY

The coordination difficulties in children with ADD affect the whole range of coordination. These children are likely to have problems with gross motor coordination, fine motor coordination, eye/hand and eye/foot coordination. The most common disability is in the area of fine motor co-ordination.

In addition, these children invariably have what is known as crossed dominance. This is the state where the child prefers to use, for instance, the right hand for certain activities and the left hand for other activities. The child may use the right eye preferentially but be left-handed, and even possibly right-footed. In effect, there is no established dominance of one side of the body over the other. Most people tend to be either right dominant or left dominant. About 95 per cent of the world's population is left hemispheric dominant which means that they are right-handed, right-eyed and right-footed. A small percentage are right hemispheric dominant and therefore left-handed. An even smaller percentage have some permanent mixed dominance. They are the people with permanent ambidexterity.

Crossed dominance has a high incidence in children with ADD and appears only to resolve itself when the affected part of the brain undergoes maturation in adolescence. Until then, these are the children who tend to mix their knives and forks up when they are eating and possibly write with their right hands and play tennis or cricket with their left hands.

Many people have taken this crossed dominance as being the cause of learning difficulties rather than as an accompanying feature. As a result, some therapies have arisen using the concept of the so-called "split brain". This presupposes that one half of the brain is responsible for language function and the other half controls music, mathematics and other non-verbal tasks. The therapies then purport to return function to the appropriate parts of the brain by a range of physical exercises, training techniques, etc. Quite clearly, the basis for these therapies is false as we know that there is a great interconnection between the two hemispheres and that a particular function is not neatly located in only one area of the brain.

Children with coordination difficulties are best managed by an occupational therapist or physiotherapist. These professionals are trained to provide the uncoordinated child with a range of exercises which would improve the specific functions that are poorly developed. Consequently, the child may engage in what is called a gross motor, fine motor, or eye/hand control program.

Gross motor programs include functions such as trampolining, rolling with large balls, and exercising in an adventure playground. Fine motor programs are geared at improving the child's fine manipulative skills with a whole range of exercises such as putting pegs in holes, or threading needles. Eye/hand coordination is improved by constant practice with catching skills and judging distances in throwing balls, and similarly with kicking.

Occupational therapy programs usually run for a period of twelve weeks with review sessions at regular intervals.

DIETARY CONTROL

Much has been written about the effects of diet upon the child with ADD, especially those with a hyperactive nature. I think most people are familiar with the book written by Dr Ben Feingold regarding the dietary management of the hyperactive child. The basis of this book was Dr Feingold's experience with adult patients and their reaction to certain foods in the management of their allergic conditions. This was then further extended to the treatment of children with allergic conditions and, subsequently, children with hyperactivity. The diet was put forward as a panacea for a whole host of conditions, of which the hyperactivity was the most notable.

Various research articles have been published where clinical trials have been conducted on dietary management, such as the Feingold Diet, in the management of children with hyperactivity. Almost without exception these studies have found no significant benefit from diet in the control of hyperactivity. This is probably true for the parameters that were used in those research studies. However, I have been singularly impressed by numerous parents who have found significant improvement in their children with the withdrawal of certain food substances from their diet. Commonly involved foods are cocoa derivatives such as chocolate and cola drinks. Other frequently noxious foodstuffs include preservatives, food colourings and sugar. Salicylates have also been incriminated.

How do you compare the individual experiences of various parents with those of the clinical trials? In a clinical trial, certain parameters are used to categorise the child as being hyperactive. These children are viewed only at certain times and observations made in particular circumstances. The parents, however, have to live with the child twenty-four hours a day and their experiences are therefore of a much fuller nature. There are certain qualitative hazards of a hyperactive child which are not frequently noted in the quantitative studies that are done. The mood swings of these children, as well as their aggression and impulsiveness, often do not come through on standardised psychological testing, especially in the artificial environments in which they are performed.

My advice to parents of children with hyperactivity is to exercise some control over the diet and to ensure that there is no excess of the foodstuffs that I have mentioned above.

In the younger children, I suggest that they try an elimination diet for a few weeks and, if there is an improvement in the child (usually this is in the form of better sleep patterns or reduced activity levels) then they should continue. If after a few weeks there is no improvement, then I recommend that they cease the elimination diet.

One of the concerns with an elimination diet is that many children see it as being punitive and, for that reason, usually the whole family has to engage in this form of therapy so that the child does not feel that he is being singled out. The hyperactive child may tend towards paranoia as a side effect of this dietary management.

DRUG THERAPY

Treatment of children with ADD with drug therapy is both the most controversial and the most successful form of management for these children.

The history of drug therapy dates back to 1937 when Dr Bradley, a researcher in the United States, was investigating a new drug called Dexamphetamine which was thought to improve the headaches that children experienced after being subjected to an investigation known as pneumoencephalography. Pneumoencephalography is a technique in which air is injected into a child's central nervous system and X-rays taken to determine whether there is any tumour in the brain. The procedure is no longer used as the CAT scan has now superseded this. One of the major side effects of pneumoencephalography is a profound headache after the procedure.

Dexamphetamine was thought to possibly have benefit in improving this symptom. A controlled trial was done with a group of children over a six-month period using Dexamphetamine in 1937. Unfortunately, no improvement was found as far as the headaches were concerned, but it was noticed that a number of these children who were experiencing learning difficulties prior to the trial had improved significantly in their learning at the end of the trial. From this point, Dexamphetamine was further investigated as a treatment for children with learning difficulties, especially as a result of Minimal Brain Dysfunction.

It did not take long for Dexamphetamine to become established as a form of treatment for children with learning difficulties resulting from Minimal Brain Dysfunction. About two decades later, a new drug was released named Methylphenidate (trade name Ritalin). This was thought to be an improvement upon Dexamphetamine as it had fewer side effects and seemed to afford a better control of children with Minimal Brain Dysfunction. Its effect upon the child with hyperactivity was quickly noted and, in the 1950s, various clinical studies were performed which found that Ritalin was an excellent treatment for a hyperactive child.

At present, all but a small percentage of children with ADD respond to either of these drugs. Of those who do not respond, several are actually made worse by the drugs. Others respond to medication such as Tofranil, whose mode of action is not fully understood. For this reason all children being evaluated for possible treatment should have a laboratory assessment of their response to that particular drug prior to the initiation of treatment.

(a) Mode of Action

One of the frustrating features about the new medications

was the fact that it was not understood how they performed their tasks. It later became clear that in adults who received these medications the effect was either to cause some depression or to elevate their mood.

As the medications became more widely known among the public they tended to be abused by adults who found they were habit-forming. Despite this, the medications continued to be used in the clinical situation in children with hyperactivity, and with marked success. Study after study indicated the significant benefits to the child with hyperactivity when treated with these medications.

At first, the effects of Ritalin and Dexamphetamine were thought to have a "paradoxical effect" upon children as they appeared to work in the opposite direction to adults. In other words, overactive children tended to be slowed down and settled on the medication whereas normal adults had a "speeding up" effect in which they received the so-called "high" or altered state.

As the mode of action of these drugs in the child with Minimal Brain Dysfunction or hyperactivity was unknown, control studies were initiated to monitor if there were any side effects. So far, there have been several long-term studies, the most notable being conducted at the Montreal Children's Hospital by Dr Weiss in which a group of children was treated with these drugs for five years in the late 1950s. At the end of their treatment period the medications were discontinued and the children reviewed on a five yearly basis. There were also two control groups: an untreated group and a group of children who did not have Minimal Brain Dysfunction. The most recent report on these children is the 20 year follow-up study which has not reported any long-term side effects in the treated group. The outcome of the three groups has been best in the children who did not have ADD. The next best outcome was in the group with ADD who received treatment with the drug therapy and the least successful outcome was in the untreated group.

Only in the last five to ten years has the suspected mode of action of these medications become apparent. I repeat here the diagram shown in the earlier chapter on the origin of this condition. You will recall that the basic underlying problem in ADD is a dysfunction of the neurotransmitter, which is the chemical that relays impulses from one cell to the next. The neurotransmitters involved were dopamine and noradrenaline.

The chemical compositions of Methylphenidate (or Ritalin), Dexamphetamine (Dexedrine) and Pemoline (Cylert) are very similar to those of the natural substances themselves. It appears that the likely mode of action of these medications is multi-directional. Firstly, they afford a straight-forward increase in the level of the neurotransmitter in the gap between the two nerve cells and in this way act as neurotransmitters themselves. Secondly, they decrease the re-uptake of the natural neurotransmitter into the first cell which further increases the amount of neurotransmitter in the gap between the cells.

A third mode of action is to improve the receptiveness of the membrane of the second cell for the natural neurotransmitter, so increasing the affinity of the second cell for the neurotransmitter, attracting it almost like a magnet. A fourth action is to interfere with the enzyme system which destroys the natural neurotransmitters.

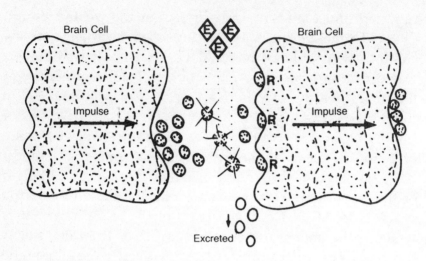

In children with ADD
(brain cells in affected area)

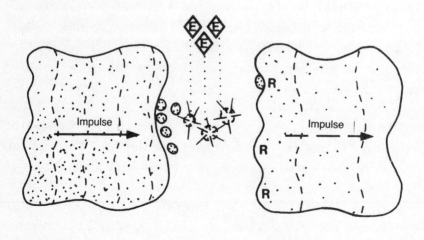

 Neurotransmitter (Cell fluid)

Inactive Neurotransmitter

 Enzyme

R Receptor

The result of any therapy is to improve the transmission of the electrical impulse from the first cell to the second cell and, subsequently, through the nervous system. Quite logically, if a person has normal levels of neurotransmitter and there is no significant difficulty, then these medications would enhance the transmission of impulses above what is normal and this leads to the side effects experienced by adults who do not have ADD.

(b) Side Effects

The side effects of these medications are short-term. Generally, the younger the child, the more significant the side effects. The most common one is appetite loss which, in the young child, can last anywhere from several weeks to several months. As a result, there is a risk of weight loss and I have seen some children lose between 3 and 4.5 kg (7 and 10 lb) within the first few months. However, the weight then usually reaches a stable point and there is a general increase thereafter. A quicker way of regaining the weight is to withdraw the treatment for a short period until the child's weight and appetite improve. In many cases, when the medication is recommenced, there is not the significant weight loss experienced with the first administration of the medication. However, these children do complain of a certain fullness in the stomach and that is one of the reasons why they do not eat their lunch at school, or even their breakfast in the morning.

The next most common side effect is insomnia and a large number have difficulty in falling asleep when treatment is initiated. Again, this side effect is more prominent in the younger child as opposed to the older child. Eventually, the child adjusts to the medication and the insomnia improves in virtually all cases.

Other side effects include some initial fatigue, occasional headaches, occasional dizziness and, in exceptional cases, some blurring of vision. All these side effects usually do not last for more than a few days before they dissipate as the child adjusts to the medication.

There was one report in 1972 in which it was thought that there was some effect upon the linear growth in children who were treated with these medications. However, this initial report has not been substantiated by various other researchers, and I certainly have not seen, in over 5000 cases that I have treated in the last ten years, any linear growth retardation in a child with ADD who is on treatment with these drugs. That original study indicated that the children whom they suspected of having linear growth retardation, were able to regain their growth appropriately when the medication was withdrawn. In 1979, the American Academy of Paediatrics published a statement in one of the medical journals indicating that there was no concrete evidence that growth retardation was a side effect of drug therapy in children with ADD.

A side effect that is frequently seen in the very young child who commences medication is an initial depression. Where the child is under the age of seven, he could frequently suffer tearfulness, irritability and increased tension for a few weeks while adjusting to the medication. Invariably, these symptoms can be improved with a reduction in the dosage.

Tofranil appears to have few lasting side effects. Some children may have initial drowsiness or increased appetite.

Almost without exception, the child who responds to drug therapy responds with greater success to all other therapies that are being applied. In other words, when one has improved the internal environment in the child's brain, the child responds much more appropriately to the other therapies that are designed to improve his external environment.

KEY POINTS
- Behavioural therapy moves the child from negative towards positive experiences.
- Remedial education uses the child's academic strengths while supporting the weaknesses.
- Speech therapy should treat problems with speech as well as language.
- Occupational therapy improves the following:
  1. Gross motor coordination
  2. Fine-motor coordination
  3. Eye/hand coordination
  4. Handedness
  5. Progression from left to right
  6. Visuo-spatial problems
- Diet tries to eliminate foods that further diminish neurotransmitter function.
- Drugs (Ritalin, Dexedrine, Pemoline) modify the disordered neurochemistry in the brain.

CHAPTER 17

MANAGEMENT AND THE OTHER THREE R'S

This chapter gives a general introduction to managing the child's external environment. A child with ADD needs both neurological treatment and environmental supervision.

It is essential to accept that almost all these children have great difficulty with organisational skills. They are disorganised people who depend upon the environment to afford them some form of structure both at home and at school.

At home, the child with ADD needs a very strict routine in daily activities. He needs to do each activity at a set time on each day and these activities should be done with great regularity. In other words, what is done at 8 o'clock today is done at 8 o'clock tomorrow.

One of the greatest problems the school child with ADD has is homework and study. He has little idea or inclination of how to arrange his time after school so that homework is included. He should be assisted in drawing up an after-school program for each day of the week, and divide the time into half-hour slots. Each slot should then be allocated an activity such as snacktime, play, homework, study, television, dinner, bathtime, etc. He should then be encouraged to stick to this timetable as strictly as possible. Initial monitoring would be necessary to help him into this routine.

This sort of program breaks the afternoon and evening

up and provides variety, while at the same time the home-work gets done.

In addition, because of short-term memory difficulties, he needs to have instructions and information provided repeatedly.

You will notice that I am emphasising three important "Rs" as well as the three "Rs" that they should be learning. For the child with ADD, the three "Rs" of routine, regularity and repetition are just as crucial as the basic three "Rs" (reading, writing and arithmetic).

There should also be great consistency of management and very little chopping and changing in the ground rules of the home. The home environment should be a fairly stable and quiet one, with noise kept to a minimum.

Due to their low self-esteem and their lack of security, these children need constant reassurance that they are accepted as they are and are also part of the family community. It is very important that fathers play a large role in the rearing of these children. Boys with ADD, because of the various emotional difficulties, are constantly testing the limits of discipline and control and it is very difficult for the mother, who may be in the front line, to constantly meet these challenges. The regular input of a father into not only the behavioural management but also the emotional development of the child is important. Children with ADD are, in most cases, physical people who require a lot of demonstration of physical love and affection. When they have transgressed, the punishment should be swift and fair and the matter resolved straight away.

KEY POINTS
- ADD children require a strict routine for daily activities.
- Information needs to be frequently repeated before the ADD child stores it in memory.
- Exposure to information should be at regular intervals.

CHAPTER 18

SPECIFICS OF MANAGEMENT

BEHAVIOURAL DISORDERS

Children with ADD (especially the ones with hyperactivity) have a variety of behavioural features which distinguish them from other children. Many children display aspects of these behavioural disorders at one time or another but in the hyperactive child they persist over an extended period of time and are often resistant to disciplinary intervention.

TEMPER TANTRUMS

Because the child with ADD is a rather inflexible person, he finds it very difficult to adjust to changes in his environment. The establishment of an unchanging environment would be unrealistic as these children would be presented at some stage or other with having to deal with an alteration in their customary routine. The low frustration level that many seem to have leads to frequent explosions of temper in a changing environment. In many cases, these outbursts of temper appear to have no obvious point of provocation and the parents are almost dumbfounded as to what is the cause of the child's temper tantrum. It can be as insignificant as the fact that the mother has not buttered the bread right to the ends of the slice.

The child explodes in an uncontrollable fashion which can last several minutes but usually no longer than about ten to fifteen minutes. One of the characteristics of the temper outburst is that it is fairly short-lived. During that time, the best course for the parent is to remove his or her own personal involvement from the episode. Not becoming personally involved in the outburst is one of the most difficult things to do but also one of the most successful. The child should be removed from the causative area and preferably placed in a secluded room which would afford him the opportunity to settle down. This is the age-old time-out technique. It has been shown that these children seem to settle down much quicker if they are placed in a room which can be locked.

Some parents find it successful in restraining the child during a temper outburst by embracing him and holding him fairly tightly until the violence of the outburst has subsided. The closeness and comforting nature of the parent's body is frequently used as a catalyst in settling the child down, as long as he does not have the feeling that he is being smothered.

Once the child has settled down, he can be reasoned with more fruitfully. Obviously, this is not a technique that can be used when the mother is in the supermarket and the child is spinning himself around the floor screaming like a jumbo jet ready for take-off. In these situations the only, although not completely satisfactory, device is to ignore the child and continue with the shopping expedition for as long as possible, before returning to the car or home with the child following behind or holding him by the hand. It is essential that the child be shown that the temper tantrum will not result in any immediate gain for him.

One of the features of inflexibility is the great difficulty in handling choice. The best rule is never to allow them choice but always to present them with a *fait accompli*. They should be told which clothes to put on, where to go, how to do it, what to eat, etc. Choice is not yet something that can be placed on the social menu for these children.

AGGRESSION

Many hyperactive boys can be aggressive, especially towards their siblings or parents. The aggression is another outflow of the low frustration threshold and it is probably also one way of their being able to express some comment upon their environment and the difficulties they have in coping with it.

The element of aggression is, in many instances, the most disabling feature of ADD as far as the mother is concerned. The acts of aggression perpetrated by her child quickly rebound upon her as the frontline of defence. After a while the boy earns a bad name ("Give a dog a bad name and it sticks"). This results in the child receiving the blame, automatically, for any disturbance at school or in the neighbourhood, whether or not he was involved.

Eventually, the mother feels restricted to her home and endeavours to restrict the child as well, leading to further withdrawal from the community.

Handling aggression is very difficult and, certainly, it should not be countered by aggression. Corporal punishment of a child who has been aggressive often inflames the situation rather than douses it. By and large, the best method is the withdrawal of privileges and some form of positive reward for good behaviour. This should be engaged in with regard to the rest of the family, so that the other children do not feel that the hyperactive child is obtaining some form of material gain as a result of his aggression.

If the aggression is of such a nature that the well-being of the siblings or neighbours is being threatened, then the offending child should be separated and banished to his room for the recreational hours of the day. Once he has earned his right to re-enter the family unit, he can achieve this in a measured or step-like fashion.

Fortunately, the actual aggressive act is a fairly short-lived outburst but it can have serious consequences for the structure of the family as a whole, often severely limiting the social interaction of other family members.

SELF-ESTEEM

Diminished self-esteem can be the most intractable feature to deal with in children with ADD. As has been mentioned, the self-esteem difficulty is due to dysfunction in the limbic forebrain. Consequently, these children start off life having a diminished concept of themselves and their worthiness among their peer group. As the child enters infant school this is not always evident but certainly will become more established by the time he enters primary school in year 3 or 4.

These children have increasing difficulties in relating to other children of their own age, as they do not have confidence within the peer group. They are inclined to withdraw from a group, or else become very domineering and bossy, attempting to control their peer group. There is a greater impetus to mix with older or younger children where they feel more at ease.

Their self-esteem can only be improved when the child achieves some form of success, either on the academic or social front. If they experience learning disabilities, secondary self-esteem problems result which further compound the situation. For that reason, learning disabilities, should they occur, should be attended to immediately in an effort to restore the child's self-confidence.

The parent should also be on the constant lookout for some area in which the child demonstrates ability. The children with ADD who do discover some field of activity where they can perform relatively well, invariably improve their self-esteem in childhood. Exploring activities such as scouting, sports, dancing, acting or theatre work, debating skills, ability to build models, or computer skills, are not only essential but must be relentless. Success in any extramural activity would enhance the child's abilities to conduct himself within the social situation in the peer group.

Children with ADD are usually more at ease with one or two friends than in a group situation. Therefore, whenever they have friends over to play, or parties, these should be kept to the smallest number possible. One could almost say that when they are having someone to play, it should be one other child and no more.

As adolescence approaches, their self-esteem is again under threat as are all children at this stage. The child with ADD just suffers it more significantly. If, by that stage, he has already achieved some form of success in his childhood, he is usually in a better situation to cope with the onslaught of puberty. The low self-esteem caused by ADD improves quite considerably when the limbic system matures, usually in mid to late adolescence.

IMPULSIVENESS

Probably the most disabling feature of ADD in the long term is the impulsiveness. One of the best ways of countering impulsiveness in the young child, is to establish a very fixed routine for him as soon as possible. Good routine frees the child to concentrate on other aspects of development (learning, socialisation, etc.) and also allows him to become used to a structured way of life. Routine is so important in the life of a child with ADD that, without it, he will encounter great difficulty in overcoming his problems.

He should also be encouraged to think carefully before he proceeds with any activity, whether physical, written or spoken. It may even be useful to place little signs stating, "Think before you leap" and arrange these at strategic points, such as above his bed, in the school bag, on the desk at school and various other places. This then has the facility of flashing a message into his subconscious which eventually would be useful as a check mechanism before he engages in any impulsive activity.

Naturally, the very young child has to be watched with great vigilance as they are dangerous to themselves, particularly, but also to others. Their penchant for running across the road without looking, or jumping off high buildings, is notorious. There are countless other hazards for the young child and it would be necessary for the parent to be ever vigilant, although this is very taxing. The child himself is blissfully unaware of the distress he causes as he goes about executing what appears to be a death wish.

As the child gets older, the impulsiveness takes its form in different ways. The child is impulsive in his schoolwork, where he often assumes he knows what is being taught or required of him and then proceeds with his schoolwork quite erroneously. They often jump the gun in question time or at examinations.

Impulsiveness also manifests itself in naughty pranks at school and they are very easily led by others who would rather set up the ADD child, than be caught out themselves. The ADD child gives no thought to the consequences of his actions and invariably is the one left in the invidious position when the teacher comes along. This can become much more serious when, to gain recognition in his peer group socially, he often is led to perform criminal activities such as thieving and vandalising.

It is necessary, at regular intervals, as he is growing up, to make him aware of his impulsiveness and to encourage him to develop some form of strategy to check this impetuosity. I mentioned the notices for the young child which leave a subliminal message in his brain helping him check this impulsiveness.

As the child gets older, the consequences of his impulsiveness must be explained to him. However, the most successful form of management is to ensure that the child is not placed in situations of temptation or where he is at risk, or to try to reduce these situations as much as possible. Parents are, therefore, required always to be one or two steps ahead of the child in anticipating the possible outcome of certain ventures or even the activities of the playmates that he has selected. Unfortunately, many of these children tend to be attracted to the sort of child who would have quite the wrong influence upon them.

ATTENTION SPAN DIFFICULTIES

The most ubiquitous feature of ADD is the symptom which has given it its name. The children invariably have either a brief attention span or have difficulty in focusing their concentration upon any given task. For the parent and the teacher, there are really only two ways in which to overcome this difficulty. Firstly, the child should be freed of distractions as much as possible. In the classroom, he should be placed at the front of the class in the centre, right under the eyes of the teacher where he can, with little effort, be brought back to task as his mind wanders. So also, at home, when he does homework or any form of academic pursuit, he should be in a separate room where he is completely free of distractions or interruptions.

Secondly, work or activities that are presented to these children should be for fairly brief periods of time. An example of this is the excellent children's program, *Sesame Street*. It is geared to the attention span of the two to five-year-old and no activity lasts for more than a few seconds, usually thirty seconds at the most. Consequently, the children maintain their interest and are able to sit through a half-hour program with enjoyment, which they otherwise would not have been able to do. This is the technique to be used for the child with an attention span problem.

A result of the diminished concentration is that these children are great procrastinators. They always put off until later what they could really be doing at the present moment. As a rule, their homework, as well as their schoolwork, suffers and they have great difficulty in settling down to initiate and complete their work. In this regard, the parent can often be of assistance in helping the child to settle down in the afternoon to commence homework. Various strategies could be used, such as making the work environment attractive and conducive to work, and also to put forward little reward systems for the initiation and completion of the homework. For instance, the child could be told that if he starts his homework then, a short while later, he could have some hot chocolate or milk or another drink. At the completion of the homework there is the prospect of a snack or some sort of delight for the child. Children, and boys in particular, are usually easily bribed by way of their stomach especially where these bribes include treats that are not otherwise available

The initial enthusiasm for a project or hobby is usually followed by a rapid waning of the interest level. Gentle but persistent nagging is often necessary to get the child to complete tasks, as he must acquire the habit of sticking to things. I call it "stickability". In fact, children with ADD usually leave behind them a record of unfinished projects. The important thing is to get him into the habit of starting and finishing some set task. It does not matter whether the initial task is only brief, this can be expanded as the child becomes more used to the manner of starting and completing work.

EVALUATING DRUG THERAPY

Drug therapy is considered for children who have ADD in the following instances:

(a) Children with a moderate form of ADD, in other words those who are experiencing mild to moderate difficulties with learning or behaviour, will be considered for medication when a period of management involving either remedial tuition or behavioural therapy has been exercised for approximately four to six months. During this period, if the child is not showing significant improvement as a result of the remedial tuition or the behavioural therapy, then medication is considered.

(b) Children who have had severe forms of learning difficulties or behavioural disorders, in other words who are more than three years behind their age level with their basic skills, or are developing significant problems in behaviour either at school or at home, to the point that the school teacher or the parents are no longer able to cope, will be considered for medication upon the first interview with the physician. The clinical response to medication would then be evaluated and, should the child respond to the drug, treatment would take place in conjunction with the remedial teaching or the behavioural therapy program.

It is essential to establish at the outset whether a particular child will benefit from one of the psychostimulant drugs. Not all children with ADD respond to the medication and, in fact, a small proportion actually experience adverse effects. In this group of children, their condition actually gets worse when they are placed on the medicine and their learning deteriorates, or their behaviour becomes more chaotic.

Assessment of a child's response to treatment may take various forms but should be conducted within the controlled situation of the clinical office. Basically, you assess the child's abilities in short-term memory and attention prior to the administration of one of the medications. Then wait for a period of one to two hours for the medicine to be absorbed and circulated through the bloodstream in the brain.

After that interval the child's short-term memory and attention can be assessed once more to determine whether there has been a significant improvement in these faculties. Should this be the case, then the child is considered to be an appropriate responder to the medication and a trial course of the treatment can be undertaken for a few months. A review is usually necessary after three to six months of the treatment.

When the drug therapy is evaluated in this way it is possible to eliminate the children who are non-responders, or even adverse responders, to the medicine. In this fashion, the side effects are lessened to a considerable extent.

The child under medication has to be reviewed on a regular basis, initially either at three or six months and then, after that, at six monthly intervals. At each review an assessment has to be done of the learning progress if this were the problem, or an evaluation of the child's progress in the behavioural sphere if this were the major difficulty. Should the child also be receiving some form of speech therapy, occupational therapy or dietary control, then it is very useful in the total management of the condition to receive reports from these various professionals regarding the child's progress.

The point at which the drugs are withdrawn depends on various factors. If the problem is essentially that of a learning difficulty, then the drug therapy can be withdrawn as soon as the child has resolved his deficiency and consolidated his basic skills. In some cases, children will need to continue with the medication as their attention deficit severely interferes with their abilities to progress in high school. These children will require treatment until they essentially grow out of the condition.

With behavioural problems the child requires medicine until an improved behavioural pattern has been established and maintained. Once this is effected, the medication may be withdrawn for a trial period. In most cases, treatment is necessary until the condition undergoes natural resolution.

Monitoring the dynamics of the ADD is a fairly difficult task. The advent of computerised assessments (Neurometrics or BEAM) have facilitated these reviews and it is much easier now to establish at which stage the child is starting to resolve the neurological dysfunction and can, therefore, be withdrawn from his drug therapy program.

Should the facility of a computerised neurological assessment not be available, then the next best is the "hit and miss" method. The child is periodically withdrawn from his medicine for a period of one term. If there is no significant decline in his performances he is kept off the medication until there appears to be a difficulty. Should the child be off his medicine for more than six months, and not have encountered significant problems, then it can be accepted that he has either resolved the condition or is able to compensate for the difficulties.

When the psychostimulant drugs are used in a structured, ordered and controlled way, the benefits are often incalculable for the particular child and the side effects negligible. It is only the children who have no benefit, or are adversely affected by the medication, who will not be considered for the drug therapy.

KEY POINTS
- Temper tantrums are best managed by allowing the child to regain control of his emotions.
- Aggression is improved by reward and withdrawal of privileges.
- Impulsiveness can be reduced by developing effective strategies.
- Attention span may be improved by:
  1. Distraction-free environment
  2. Shorter working periods
  3. Varying work content
  4. Rewards for finishing tasks
- Drug therapy is evaluated by measuring response of attention/short-term memory to medication.

CHAPTER 19

ADD AND THE NUCLEAR FAMILY

As the poet John Donne stated, "No man is an island unto himself". The child with ADD does not live in isolation and his behaviour has an effect upon the people in his immediate environment and, likewise, the reactions of the people immediately about him have an effect upon him.

The nuclear family is crucial to the development of the child with ADD. It has been my experience that the child who is in a family where there are strong ties between the various members and especially a stable relationship between the mother and father, is more likely to overcome his difficulties in the long run.

I have mentioned earlier that children with ADD need to be managed with a very steady routine as well as consistency and discipline. The home that provides this for the child is also the one that will provide him with the route to success in overcoming his ADD.

The relationships within the family can be reduced to four factors and they are of decreasing importance. Firstly, the relationship between the mother and the father; then the relationship between the mother and the child; the relationship between the father and the child; and the relationship between the child and his or her siblings.

FATHER AND MOTHER
If the relationship between the father and the mother is not a strong one, this would have serious consequences for all

children. Children, in a home where the father and mother either do not love each other or only tolerate each other for the sake of the children, soon learn the cold comforts of a loveless home. The child with ADD has a much greater need for a solid basis, or grounding, in his life and also to know that he is loved within the home and that the love comes from the love that exists between the parents. Discord between parents kills the hearts of all children, but in the child with ADD it also numbs their senses. The majority of them already start off life with diminished abilities to display emotion and, in some cases, lack depth of emotion. They may be people who do not develop appropriate self-confidence and self-esteem. Family discord will just exaggerate this personality difficulty and entrench it for many years, if not decades.

The child with ADD also develops a greater cunning than the normal child in utilising the discord between his parents to his advantage. Should the parents not be able to present a united front to the child with ADD, then the descent down the crater into the volcano has already commenced. As the child becomes more accustomed to manipulating either parent against the other, he will experience greater problems in relating to the outside world where his manipulative techniques will not be tolerated. Eventually, this leads to his greater isolation.

At the same time, the child with ADD places enormous strain upon the relationship between the parents which, at many times, will reach breaking point. The mother is often with the child all day and has to cope with his onslaughts of overactivity and impulsiveness, lying and cheating, as well as his interaction with other children and the reactions that she receives from neighbours and school teachers. The father, on the other hand, in many cases is at work all day and returns home for some quiet, rest and comfort as well as some delight in the family to which he is looking forward to rejoining.

When the father arrives home, the mother welcomes him with the news that the child has committed another one of his trangressions and her nerves are raw. He is thrown into a maelstrom of confused emotions and has to use all the managerial skills that, very likely, he has been busy with all day to solve the problem at home. This is often not satisfactorily done, as the period between 5 o'clock in the afternoon and 8 o'clock at night is a period when most people are at their lowest ebb and it is also the period of greatest risk in any home situation.

As a result of the constant confrontations when he arrives home, the father chooses to arrive home a little bit later each night, hoping in this way to avoid the unpleasantness and difficulties. Gradually, and insidiously, he removes himself from the family and, eventually, also from his wife. She, on the other hand, feels deserted and unsupported in having to manage this difficult child and invariably starts to shift part of the blame from the child to her husband.

It has been well established that in the family where there is an ADD child with hyperactivity, there is almost a third higher instance of marital discord and breakdown than in the normal population.

Where the parents are already separated, the task is all the more onerous. In many cases, the parents have separated under less than amicable terms, and are often barely on speaking terms with each other. This makes the management of the child with ADD more difficult as each parent invariably becomes a unit within him or herself. The single parent usually has to assume the roles of both father and mother, further exhausting his/her resources. In many instances, the parents play the child off against each other and I have seen cases where one parent, in order to frustrate the other parent, will deliberately contradict the principles of management that have been exercised by the other parent. The parent who has custody of the child is in a more invidious position, as there is no respite at all from the child's behaviour and no one else to call upon to take over when the resources have run low.

Both parents have to realise that the child's difficulty is something that they need to deal with as a unit and a team, and that it will be causing endless frustrations and disappointments along the way. During the years that they are managing the condition they will change very much, both in their perceptions and management of children, as well as in their perceptions of professionals who offer advice and assistance.

In most of the families that I have seen where there is a child with ADD, it has been a common experience that the parents, having decided that there is something different about their child, seek recourse to one or another professional group. In many cases, they are either told that the child is normal and that he will grow out of his difficulties, or that they are not managing him correctly and various methods of management are then suggested. They may even be informed that all the boy needs is some good old-fashioned discipline — probably a beating.

As they move from professional to professional, with

little improvement in the situation, they acquire a reputation of either being parents who feel that their child should be better than he is, or are just plain neurotic. Some parents are fortunate and gain the ear of a sympathetic professional fairly early on, who is able to guide them in the correct direction for the proper management of their child. Others are not so lucky.

The fact remains that the road to eventual success in managing the child with ADD, is a long and arduous one and not always easy to follow. However, it is one that must be followed as a team for, disunited, everyone will fail.

I think one of the most significant blocking mechanisms to the successful outcome of a family with a child with ADD is the fact that the parents do not recognise that they have to go into a mourning process for the normal child that they do not have. All of us, when we start off our families, look forward with eagerness and anticipation and planning to the new child's arrival, and the improved prospects we would like to provide for that child. The glossy magazines encourage us to gain an image of a child being born in misty splendour and that, from then on, it is plain sailing, giving the impression that raising a healthy, obedient, bright child is a straightforward process.

The parents who have a child with ADD are brought to a rude awakening as far as this dream is concerned. Theirs is not the picture book child and it is essential for them to move through the different phases of the mourning process in order that they reach acceptance of the fact that theirs is a temporarily handicapped child (although one who with proper management can reach normal adulthood). Many, if not most, fathers arrest at the early stages of this mourning process and it is the mothers who advance more rapidly, probably because they are closer to nature and have instinctive feelings about the raising of their children.

Each parent needs to move through the successive phases of denial, anger, blame and withdrawal before acceptance is reached. The step that most fathers stop at is denial that the problem exists. They refuse to discuss the matter and in this way develop a relationship with a child who does not exist, while the real child has to grow up without proper parental support.

Anger is often directed at the child or the other parent, or even towards the professional who makes the diagnosis. Fortunately, this is a short-lived phase. Blame is more insidious. I have seen parents who have moved through the first two phases and appear to accept the condition but, under the surface, are constantly seeking to blame someone for the condition. This is a natural phenomenon as there are few things in life that so graphically demonstrate to us our helplessness, mortality and insignificance than to have an unwell child. We will seek out reasons and explanations but our gut feeling is that we have been poorly handled by fate.

Eventually, after having withdrawn from the family to take stock, the parent recognises the situation, resigns himself to it and at last accepts it. He is then ready to give the child his most constructive support.

Where a parent is arresting at one of the stages of the mourning process, he or she needs professional assistance to progress through to the final acceptance of the child's difficulties and it is only at that point that they are in a position to be of constructive assistance to the child and the family as a whole.

THE MOTHER

Individually, the mother is the most important factor in the life of a child with ADD. As I have indicated before, the condition of ADD is a genetic one and mostly male. This is very fortunate, as it would usually follow that the mother does not have any features of ADD. I have frequently experienced much greater difficulty in managing a child with ADD in a family where the mother also has features of the condition.

The mother of a child with ADD has little choice but to stay at home and care for the child. She frequently suffers from low self-esteem and as a result she feels she is an inferior being who serves a basic function of procreation and rearing children and, therefore, has little to offer intellectually, spiritually or financially. This overrides the view of the mother being the central figure in the family and the one who determines the ultimate outcome of her children, and even her husband.

In families where the mother is perspicacious, attentive, as well as loving, the various family members usually adjust well to society and develop normal adult lives. Where this is not the case, the opposite usually occurs. It is crucial for a child with ADD to have a mother who is aware of his difficulties, if not at a conscious level then at a subconscious level, and who is prepared to give of herself and her time to help him overcome these temporary problems.

Very early on in the child's life the mother recognises the fact that this child is different, even shortly after it is born.

Mothers soon know that the child is not developing appropriately and start to send out the early warning signals to their husbands and other family members. Eventually, they visit the doctor who, like most medical professionals, will look at the mother and child and see a well fed and healthy unit and inform the mother that she has nothing to worry about and that the child's difficulties will resolve in time. Suitably reassured, the mother returns home, only to have the nagging doubts and fears return as she observes her child's development continuing in the incorrect fashion she originally observed.

Eventually, the mother again takes her child to see perhaps another doctor, who tells her not to concern herself but he will refer her to a specialist. If the mother is lucky, she will meet a specialist in childhood disorders who is at least attentive and tries to reassure her. If she is unlucky, she will meet a specialist who will listen for a short while and then inform the mother that she is at fault for the child's behavioural difficulties and for her to return home and to start being a good mother. I have seen countless mothers in the course of my practice who have had significant emotional crises, including nervous breakdowns and recourse to alcoholism, as a result of so-called well meaning professionals informing them that they are inadequate in their mothering skills.

The brave mother eventually reaches a professional who will assist her with the child with ADD. However, by this time, she bears the scars of being called neurotic, inefficient, ineffective or displaying poor parenting skills.. The last named euphemism is a beloved one of modern day psychologists and psychiatrists and used as a "too hard basket" in many instances.

Most mothers are able to keep their equanimity in the face of all these adversities and, eventually, succeed in having their child successfully assisted by various professional groups. These women deserve our plaudits and not our insults.

The mother is usually the most able person in coping with the child's frustrations (whether due to school problems or social difficulties), to protect him when he is at risk due to impulsiveness, or being easily led by others, or to assist him with organising himself. She also can double as resource teacher after school to help him with his basic skills, engage his talents to boost his self-esteem, or deal with his temper tantrums. Her constant presence at home is a relief to the child when all else is changing at school, her communicativeness helps him to unburden his fears, desires, guilt and aggression and, above all, her love will comfort him when he really hurts.

The situation is altogether more difficult for the mother who has ADD herself. She, like her child, has difficulties with sustained attention; she may be somewhat impulsive, and also have problems with organising her home and herself. These characteristics make it more difficult for her to cope with the increased workload that the child with ADD places upon her. In many cases, these mothers also have a lowered frustration threshold and, therefore, are more likely to have periods when they feel they cannot cope at all and need some assistance from professional groups. These mothers deserve our sympathy as well as our praise, since for them the pathway is even more difficult.

My advice to students is always to listen carefully to the

mother. No matter what the paediatric problem, the mother will provide all the information and even make the diagnosis if allowed. Unfortunately, they are too often viewed with either suspicion or derision.

THE FATHER

The father's role in the management and development of a child with ADD is almost as important as the mother's. Fathers, generally, have reduced input into the development of their infant children compared to the mothers.

However, as the child grows up, the input of the father becomes much more important. Boys with ADD have an almost greater need for the care and attention and affection of their fathers. Because of their low self-esteem and lack of confidence, these children have more difficulty in developing their identities and require more consistent role models. They are also naturally capricious, impulsive and test the limits of normal discipline. Here, the father is necessary to provide the firmness, as well as fairness, that is a crucial part in the development of the child with ADD. These children need to have very strictly kept boundaries, with the boundaries being enlarged bit by bit each year. It is very difficult for the mother in the midst of all her other duties to oversee the total discipline of the child as well.

The role of the father as a disciplinarian is not that of a person who constantly metes out punishments. He is there to provide the child with the feeling that there is someone upon whom the whole family can rest in times of need. At the same time, the father is also someone who provides fun for the child and will interact with him in the form of games, sport and entertaining pastimes.

The father needs to strike a careful balance between the disciplinarian and the confidant who is there at all times when the child needs help, advice or would just like to have some fun.

Modern day business has resulted in many fathers, unfortunately, reaching their homes in the evenings well after the bedtime of their children. This situation would cause the father to have less and less involvement with his children, and this is bad news for all. However, the child with ADD suffers even more acutely from these periods of deprivation. The call that I make to all fathers to spend more time and be more available for their children, is not only for children with ADD, but for all children.

SIBLINGS

The other children within the family not only risk having some feature of ADD, given its genetic nature, but also risk some of the behavioural features of the affected child.

If the child with ADD is the oldest in the family, then it is not uncommon for the younger children to imitate his behaviour and to generally accept that the standards he sets are the ones to be followed. It is very confusing for them then, if they are reprimanded for their incorrect behaviour. This is compounded by the fact that the management of the child with ADD is somewhat different to that of the normal children in the family.

The parents need to be aware of the limitations and capabilities of the child with ADD and, therefore, discipline and punishment is measured according to these abilities. This cannot always be applied to the other children in the household and they need to be controlled as normal children usually are. An example is the incident where an ADD child is pilfering money from his mother's purse. He tends to do this repetitively and it is impossible to constantly mete out punishment or corrective discipline on each occasion. Because it is such a constant feature, the parents can often only remind the child that it is an incorrect procedure and warn of the consequences that would occur should it continue into adulthood. However, if one of the other children then pilfers from the purse, he or she will usually receive the appropriate reprimand or correction. That child may then find some inequality in the management of their transgression as compared to that of the child with ADD. There will be several situations such as these and, as the other children get older, they are more able to understand the parents when they inform them that the child with ADD has a particular difficulty and, therefore, cannot always be treated in the same way as the other children.

Having said this, it is necessary to treat the child with ADD as much as possible in the same way as the other children are treated in the family. For the sake of harmony, in most instances, fairness and justice should be seen to be done in order to encourage better sibling relationships between the siblings and the child with ADD. However, all the family members come to a subconscious realisation that one of them has limited abilities to cope with certain situations and, therefore, allowances should be made. In this regard, the child with ADD could be regarded as a handicapped child but one who does not have a visible physical handicap.

KEY POINTS
- A stable home environment allows for more successful management of ADD.
- Parents need to mourn the temporary loss of the expected normal child.
- Each parent should have equal input into the child's management.
- Reassurance of siblings that they are not neglected because of the ADD child.

CHAPTER 20

THE BOY IS FATHER OF THE MAN

Virtually for all the time that research was being done into the condition of ADD, it was assumed that this was a condition that affected children and resolved in middle to late adolescence. For that reason it has been referred to as a developmental condition. This is largely true and the majority of children with ADD do experience noticeable improvements during adolescence.

However, it now appears with further research that there is a significant number of children who do not experience large improvements in late adolescence, and a very small number who experience no improvement at all. These children are now being increasingly recognised as the progenitors of an adult condition that is termed ADD (residual type). This is the term now being applied to those adults who had ADD as children but have not grown out of the feature sufficiently to become indistinguishable from their peer group.

The end results in adults are influenced by two factors. Firstly, all children with ADD, whether they have been treated or not treated, will develop certain behavioural characteristics as a result of the condition which become habitual and, eventually, form part of their personality. The degree to which these character traits do ingrain themselves as part of the personality depends upon the success of the management program.

Secondly, in the small group who have no significant

improvement in their neurochemical dysfuctions, the full-blown picture continues into adulthood but is somewhat ameliorated by the ability of the adult to compensate for his difficulties and also to devise strategies for overcoming his difficulties. Children are not as efficient as adults in developing these strategies.

What are the features of the adult with ADD? Studies done at the University of California have shown that a large proportion of hyperactive children go on to develop "type A" personalities as adults. These are the people who are always busy, active and on the go, achieving or over-achieving. They find it very difficult to let up or relax and are frequently referred to as tense people who are achievement-orientated. They do experience a lot of increased muscular tension and, as a result, a lot of fatigue. They burn a lot of energy and, therefore, are people of large appetite who seem to eat well but put on little weight.

Coupled with the physical attribute, is continued difficulty with self-esteem. The ADD adult, because of his achievement orientation, generally succeeds in his chosen career and performs very well. However, due to self-doubts, he is constantly unsure as to the genuineness and the value of his performances. Even when he is consistently and generously praised for his work, he remains suspicious and feels he has failed his own high standards.

Their difficulties with auditory attention continue and these men remain poor listeners although they are definitely much improved lookers. This presents problems socially where people are introduced but their names promptly forgotten. They are still not keen readers and will not read for pleasure. If they do read, it is mainly to gain information. Recreational reading would probably include newspapers and magazines dealing with certain topics of interest. Novels are very rarely attempted. Letter writing is also a significant difficulty as written expression problems persist.

In many cases, they are excellent managers and have a talent for conceiving a general ideal (often an inspirational one) which, because of their high energy level, and inflexibility and dogmatism, they are able to pursue until realisation. There is little doubt that they are among the "doers" in the world rather than the "watchers".

Inflexibility, coupled with impulsiveness, causes many problems, both on a social and emotional level. To a large extent, they are "black and white" people who have some difficulty in coping with the varying shades of grey. They prefer to be presented with propositions or problems in stark terms and are happier with having to make concrete, cut and dried decisions. In many cases, they are imperceptive of subtle changes that occur in relationships between people and often either do not read cues or misread cues that are coming from another person in a social situation. This could have deleterious effects, both in relationships with colleagues or with their partner.

I can almost invariably spot an adult with ADD purely by the handshake. This is the person who grasps your hand firmly and squeezes it almost to a crunching stage. When seated, close observation will reveal that there is some persistent form of muscle movement. There is a shifting around in the chair, playing with a pencil or biting a pencil top; twirling shoelaces, crossing one leg over the other and moving the dependent leg; chewing something, even if it is imaginary, playing with the hands or interlocking the fingers, and so on. These people have great difficulty in re-laxing and that is one of the major causes for fatigue at the end of their daily activities.

Where, initially, many were good sleepers as children, sleep becomes an increasing problem as they grow older. Because of the nervous energy, tension and emotional difficulties due to self-esteem problems and others, sleep also tends to be somewhat tense. Usually, because of the fatigue at the end of the day, they drop off to sleep quite quickly, but then wake frequently during the night and have great difficulty in falling asleep again.

Speech can often be a telltale sign in that the adult ADD is often a very quick or rapid-fire speaker, many times slurring his speech due to running the words one into the other. A large proportion do not enunciate clearly and speak with fairly closed mouths.

In most cases, the coordination difficulties, if they exist-ed, improve through adolescence, but some still experience coordination problems as adults. They are a bit clumsy and the handwriting may not be appropriate. Handwriting dif-ficulties persist in all those who experience handwriting problems as children, but in many professions (such as doctors) it is almost an accepted art form.

Reading difficulties can be overcome by getting a junior person in the office to peruse certain manuscripts, or even his partner may assist. The secretary is there to take dicta-tion and type the letter and, in many cases, learning dis-abilities can be hidden. There are situations in which they cannot be hidden and the risk of exposure as an illiterate is ever present in the adult ADD who did not overcome his specific learning disabilities. This is one of the most disabling features in the long run as it not only affects the careers but also the long-term self-esteem of these people. I have yet to see an adult with significant specific learning disabilities who does not suffer self-esteem problems as a result of the condition. This lack of self-esteem impinges itself upon all aspects of the person's life, both professional and personal. The self-esteem affects the self-confidence which, in turn, affects the performance.

When the adult ADD starts his own family, there is a possibility of having a child with ADD. In many cases, the father, having been aware of his difficulties is able to accommodate these in his child and support him in these weaknesses. In other instances, because of inflexibility and lack of insight, the father is unable to accept the difficulty in the child and, in many cases, refuses to be reminded of his own difficulties by the problem being reincarnated in his scion. He then blocks at the denial stage of mourning, refusing to have anything to do with the difficulties of the child. Even when he accepts the difficulties, he might find it not completely within his power to support the child as is necessary because of his own shortcomings in the emotional situation.

An examination of his career reveals that the adult with ADD is, in many if not most instances, someone whose work record reflects several changes of employment. Early adulthood is characterised by frequent changes of position as the person either realises (with more experience) that the chosen career is not appropriate, or fails to sustain interest in what was thought to be, initially, an exciting career. Many of these people change their careers several times before eventually finding the correct one, usually at a time when there has been further maturation within themselves, both neurologically and emotionally. It is therefore quite logical that the child with the history of unfinished projects and hobbies grows into the adult with a track record of inability to bring projects or sets of work to proper completion. However, with maturity this does improve, if later rather than sooner.

It is my own conviction that the child with ADD (especially the hyperactive type) is the prototype of the adult "type A" personality. There is another medical condition in adult neurology which is called Benign Essential Tremor. These are adults who have a distinct tremor of the extremities, such as the hands, which is not caused by any other significant pathology and is a benign condition that is lifelong. I have seen this tremor in many fathers of children with ADD and in whom aspects of the condition are present.

It is interesting to look back into history and view some of the great achievers who had distinct features of ADD. Albert Einstein, who was to become the mathematical and scientific genius of our age, had many features pointing towards ADD. His expressive language did not start to develop until three or four years of age and he continued to have significant difficulties with expressing himself adequately, even into later childhood. He performed poorly at school and was not outstanding in any significant area. Certainly, he had no particular prowess in mathematics while he was at school, and it was said of him that he would achieve nothing of consequence in life. He found communication, either through speech or writing, difficult, and he seemed to be a slow thinker with difficulties in decision-making processes.

Ludwig Von Beethoven was to music, what Einstein was to science. He was the major revolutionary of music at the start of the Romantic period. However, as a youngster, he also had significant difficulties with the acquisition of reading and spelling, and had particular problems with his handwriting. He was notoriously short-tempered, and impulsive, often not thinking twice about a course of action which frequently ended in disaster. He had difficulties retaining relationships in the one-to-one situation, especially with members of the opposite sex, and was regarded by many as being a loner.

Leonardo Da Vinci could, as a child, do perfect mirror writing. It is said that he often wrote in mirror form to conceal secret documents. Many people regarded his mirror writing as another example of his genuis, but viewed against the background of other personality traits, it could be seen as a feature of ADD. It is well known that as an adult he had great interest in various aspects of human exploration, including art, sculpture, science, architecture and engineering. However, he found it very difficult to complete many of his projects and many well known paintings remained unfinished, or in cartoon form. Certainly, he had great manual dexterity and skill, but the cross-dominance was ever present. He was also considered a loner, and found difficulties in establishing lasting relationships with other people. One contrasts him with the other Renaissance genius Raphael, who mixed easily with other people and built up very strong friendships that lasted throughout his life.

In adolescence and early adulthood, the untreated children with ADD, especially those who are impulsive and overactive, are much at risk of developing anti-social behaviour and juvenile delinquency. Because of their self-esteem problems and impulsiveness, they are easily led into criminal situations. Many of them are destined for an adolescent history of childhood remand centres, and eventually prisons, due to their petty crimes. Studies have shown a much higher instance of anti-social and criminal behaviour in the child with ADD.

These children are also much more prone to alcohol and drug abuse, with a higher instance in this group compared to their peer group. Various studies in alcoholism have shown a distinctly increased instance of this addiction in the child with ADD, particularly in the hyperactive one.

For all of the above reasons, these children should receive management as early as possible. That should include assessment and assistance to the family in times of stress, drug therapy for the child, and appropriate remedial tuition to improve their schoolwork and, consequently, their self-esteem. Restoration of their self-esteem is one of the major features in overcoming the later behavioural difficulties. The child should also be made to feel part of, and belonging to, his family and his group, his neighbourhood, church and society. In this way he develops a firm infrastructure on which to stand and steady himself as he enters the minefield of adolescence.

It can be seen that the boy determines the outcome in the man and the proper management and treatment of this condition in childhood will result in restoration of function, not only in childhood but also in the adult.

KEY POINTS
- A small proportion of ADD children still have symptoms in adulthood.
- Adults with ADD are often high achievers.
- Social problems in the adult ADD are common.

APPENDIX

PRACTICAL MEASURES AND REMEDIAL PROCEDURES

I. **AUDITORY PROBLEMS**
- Reception and Verbal Comprehension
- Discrimination
- Memory

II. **VISUAL PROBLEMS**
- Reception
- Discrimination
- Memory

III. **MOTOR PROBLEMS**
- Gross Motor Coordination
- Fine Motor Coordination
- Body Image

IV. **SPATIAL PROBLEMS**

V. **PROBLEMS REGARDING RIGHT/ LEFT ORIENTATION**

VI. **HYPERACTIVITY**

VII. **DISTRACTION AND SHORT ATTENTION SPAN**

I. AUDITORY PROBLEMS

Auditory Reception and Verbal Comprehension

The child with auditory reception problems can hear well and his sensory receptive organs are all intact but he is unable to attribute meaning to what he hears, hence he cannot understand it. He hears the teacher's explanation of subject matter and instruction, but he cannot carry out the instructions or absorb the subject matter because he does not understand it. Students with auditory reception problems may have trouble listening or attending to auditory stimuli, comprehending the meaning of abstract words, answering yes or no to questions containing one concept, answering comprehension questions about material they have read, understanding what they hear on the tape recorder or radio, following verbal instructions, identifying objects from verbal descriptions, attaching meaning to words and discriminating among auditory stimuli.

REMEDIAL PROCEDURES

1. The child's auditory ability may improve if the teacher gives instructions in short sentences consisting of one concept only and asks the child to repeat what he has heard.

2. Warn the child that an instruction is about to follow and encourage him to listen carefully.

3. Give only one instruction at a time.

4. Provide visual stimuli where possible.

5. Simple instructions must gradually become complicated, eg (a) walk to the door; (b) walk to the door and knock;

(c) walk to the door, knock then turn the handle; and (d) walk to the door, knock, turn the handle, open the door.

6. The child has to keep his eyes tightly closed. Use a well known object to produce a sound. The child must identify the object by the sound it produces.

7. Call out a specific action. The child has to carry out the action immediately, eg clap your hands.

8. Provide the child with a blank sheet of paper and pencils or crayons in various colours. Make sure that the child can differentiate between the colours. Ask the child to draw, for instance, (a) a blue circle then (b) a blue circle and a red cross; (c) a blue circle and a red cross, then connect the blue circle and the red cross with a brown line. Numerous exercises can be developed on this theme using concepts such as below, above, less, more, and many. For example ask the child to draw a vase with less than seven red flowers and more than five.

9. Read a short story to the child a few times. Warn him every time about the question you intend to ask: (a) let him name the people in the story; (b) let him answer short questions about the story; (c) refer to a specific incident in the story, asking him to describe the actual event; (d) ask the child to repeat the story in his own words.

10. You can name three words, two of which are similar. The child immediately has to point out the odd word, eg table, chair, table, and he would have to point out chair. The number of words can be increased as the child de-

velops his auditory ability to hear and remember more differences, e g table, chair, knife, fork, table.

11. Ask the child to use mime and gestures to act out what he hears, eg the child closes his eyes, then stamps his foot on the floor, slaps his hands on his knees, presses one hand to his stomach, the other in his back. He symbolises what he sees and hears.

12. Write to dictation. Dictate short sentences to the child. He has to write without the teacher repeating the sentence. The sentences may gradually become longer.

13. Use the Language Master, which is a teaching aid commercially available from good audio visual companies.

14. Listen to a sentence and supply the correct word, eg I am thinking of a word that tells us what to eat soup with.

15. Fill in the blanks in short stories and poems.

Auditory Discrimination
Auditory discrimination means the ability to discriminate between sounds; in other words, to hear the similarities and differences between sounds. This is not to be confused with having good auditory acuity. The child can hear perfectly well but he often confuses sounds and sound combinations in words like bit, bet, pen, pin. Such children encounter many problems, especially when the phonetic reading method is employed for beginning reading. A child who confuses the difference in sound of the visual symbols "b" and "d", for instance, has endless problems when reading words containing these letters. Some general prin-

ciples that should be remembered when developing auditory discrimination include the following:

- Begin with sounds that are clearly different, eg "k", "s".
- Produce familiar sounds first.
- Move from discrimination among gross differences, eg a telephone ringing or a knock at the door; to finer discrimination, eg a telephone ringing or a door bell ringing.

REMEDIAL PROCEDURES

1. Onomatopoeia. The child must, for instance, imitate a dog barking. Always proceed to more subtle sound discrimination, eg the barking of a happy or a frightened dog.

2. Show pictures of familiar animals and objects, eg a cat, dog, bell, car, and ask the child to make the characteristic sound in each case.

3. Sound games. Produce a sound, allowing the child to guess what it symbolises.

4. Produce long or short sounds on a piano or flute. The child has to differentiate between long or short sounds by putting up his hand when he discerns a long sound.

5. Make a tape recording of sounds produced by certain familiar objects, eg a vacuum cleaner, a school bell, a train whistling. The child has to identify the sound.

6. Stand behind the child, clapping your hands four or seven or ten times. The child has to tell every time how many times you have clapped your hands. You can also use flute, piano notes, hammer, beats on the xylophone, or knocks on the door.

7. Fill pairs of opaque plastic containers of equal sizes with: (a) paper clips; (b) grains of sand; (c) dried corn; (d) raisins or grapes. Put them down in mixed order. The child has to identify the pairs with the same contents by shaking the containers.

8. Read a short nursery rhyme, two or three times. The child has to identify the rhyming words.

9. Write a number of monosyllabic words on the board. Read them out aloud to the child, eg pit, bit, bad, red. Ask the child to underline the sound appearing most frequently in the words — the vowel sounds.

10. Make a tape recording of monosyllabic words. Replay one word at slow speed, then two, three, four and five words, etc. Every time the child has to identify: (a) the beginning; (b) the middle; and (c) the end sound and write it down.

Auditory Memory

Students who have auditory memory problems have trouble remembering what they have heard. The most frequently encountered auditory memory problem is auditory sequential memory, in other words, a child's inability to remember in the correct sequence certain syllables he has heard before. He also has a short memory span, that is he has difficulty remembering what he hears or has heard, especially the sequential use of words in sentences. Sometimes the child may remember it for a short while, sometimes for a day and sometimes for a week, but he cannot remember the sequence of events he hears about long enough to learn them successfully.

REMEDIAL PROCEDURES

1. Repeat directions that they have received before attempting to follow them.

2. Take notes while trying to memorise material so that the visual and kinesthetic feedback will help the memory.

3. Listen to auditory sequences with closed eyes to see if the visual stimuli they have been receiving are interfering with their listening.

4. Practise following directions that involve several steps.

5. Practise recalling meaningful number sequences such as telephone numbers, social security numbers, addresses.

6. Memorise songs, stories and rhymes.

7. Whenever possible the child should receive instructions in writing as well.

8. Read a number of words slowly. The child must write down each word as soon as he hears it.

9. The familiar dictation method remains one of the best. The child first learns the written form, listens while it is read out to him, then writes it.

10. Use as many visual aids as possible to develop the auditory sequential memory.

11. Place five or six objects in front of the child and give a series of directions to follow, eg put the green block in Jean's lap, place the yellow flower under John's chair and put the orange ball on Joe's desk. The list can be increased as the child improves in auditory memory.

12. Ask the child to watch a television program and remember certain things, eg watch the *Wizard of Oz* tonight and tell me all the different lands that Dorothy visited.

13. Play a game, Going to the Moon, which is an update of the game of Grandmother's Trunk or Going to New York. Say, "I took a trip to the moon and took my spaceship." The next child repeats the statement but adds one item, eg helmet.

II. VISUAL PROBLEMS

Numerous studies have established that visual perception is closely related to academic performance, particularly reading. There are also some studies that have found a number of visual perception subskills to be essential. The ones that will be dealt with here are visual reception, visual discrimination and visual memory.

Visual Reception
Visual reception is the ability to gain meaning from visual symbols. Often the child with good visual acuity cannot interpret pictures or written words. Students who have visual reception problems may have trouble selecting essential clues, scanning the perceptual field in search of information, organising what is received into a recognisable whole and attaching meaning to the visual symbols that are seen.

REMEDIAL PROCEDURES
1. Pegboard designs. Reproduce coloured visual geometric

patterns to form the design on a pegboard using coloured pegs.

2. Block designs. Use wood or plastic blocks that are all one colour or have faces of different colours. Have the child match geometric shapes and build copies of models.

3. Finding shapes in pictures. Find all the round objects or designs in a picture. Find all the square objects, and so forth.

4. Bead designs. Copy or reproduce designs with beads and string, or simply place shapes in various patterns.

5. Puzzles. Have the child put together puzzles that are teacher-made or commercially made. Subjects such as people, animals, forms or letters can be cut in pieces to show the functional parts.

6. Classification. Have the child group, or classify, geometric shapes in varying sizes or colours. The figures may be cut out of wood or cardboard or be placed on small cards.

7. Rubber band designs. Have the child copy geometric configurations with coloured rubber bands stretched between rows of nails on a board.

8. Worksheets. Ditto sheets can be purchased, or teacher-made, that are designed to teach visual reception skills. Find the objects or shapes that are different, match the same objects, find objects in various spatial positions and separate the shapes and figures from the background. Some publishers put this material into workbooks.

9. Match geometric shapes. Place shapes on cards and play games requiring the matching of these shapes.

10. Collect different sizes of jars with lids. Mix the lids and have the child match the lids with the jar.

11. Dominoes. Commercial dominoes can be used, requiring the child to match the painted dots.

12. Playing cards. A deck of playing cards provides excellent teaching material to match suits, pictures, numbers and sets.

13. Letters and numbers. Visual perception and discrimination of letters is an important reading readiness skill. Games that provide opportunities to match, sort or name shapes can be adapted to letter and numbers.

14. Letter bingo. Bingo cards can be made with letters. As the letters are called the child recognises them and covers up the letters.

15. Find the missing parts. Use pictures from magazines. Cut off functional parts of the pictures. The child finds and fills in the missing parts from a group of missing parts.

16. Visual perception of words. The ability to perceive words is, of course, highly related to reading. Games of matching, sorting, grouping, tracing and drawing geometric shapes and letters could be applied to words.

17. Use illustrations when telling a story. At the end of the narration the child has to use the illustrations, repeating the story and indicating every event in the illustrations.

18. Arrange the story cards to depict the entire story in sequence.

Visual Discrimination

Visual discrimination involves the ability to recognise the similarities and differences among items. The child with visual discrimination problems is unable to discern similarities and/or differences between different words, letters, pictures, objects. The ability to visually discriminate letters and words is an essential factor in learning to read.

REMEDIAL PROCEDURES

1. Begin by teaching the child to differentiate between words, letters and objects with obvious differences, gradually introducing examples where the differences are very small.

2. A blindfolded child must, merely by feeling various objects, distinguish similarities and dissimilarities, eg a large and a small ball, a hard and a soft teddy bear. He may remain open-eyed but must examine the objects with his hands behind his back.

3. Ask the child to classify objects from large to small, thick to thin, soft to hard.

4. Ask the child to sort matching objects or words or letters.

5. Use any newspaper or magazine article. Ask the child to ring all the "a's", or any other vowel or consonant in the article. Later, letter combinations like "nd", "ed", or "dan", can be ringed and, still later, words beginning with or ending on specific letters. Every day the child can bring his own newspaper clipping for this exercise.

6. The teacher can make sheets of nonsense words. The child can be given certain times in which to read through and circle "a's" or "b's", or whichever letter he is experiencing difficulty with. A record can be kept of the number of errors or letters that he has left out, as well as the time he has taken to complete each exercise, and this can be used to motivate him to improve on both the accuracy and the time that he has taken.

7. One can get the child to find hidden figures, letters, words or numbers in pictures.

Many of the activities listed under visual reception will be of benefit when also used in this area of visual discrimination.

Visual Memory
Students who have visual memory problems may have trouble retaining or recalling visual experiences. The most common visual memory problem is visual sequential memory. The child with visual sequential memory problems cannot remember the sequence of certain objects, letters in a word, or digits in a number, or words in a sentence he has seen. A child with this difficulty often has reading problems because he cannot visualise well.

REMEDIAL PROCEDURES
1. Use auditory method to help solve the problem, eg let the child spell the word aloud while attempting to write it down.

2. Use flash card words to develop memory. This will help him move away from entirely phonetic spelling. Decrease

the time exposure for the cards. Have him write down what he has seen.

3. Allow the pupil to look out of the window for one minute then ask him to write down three objects that he has observed. Later he can write down more.

4. Arrange pictures, objects, letters or numbers in a specific order. Allow the child to study it well. Make him turn his back while you make an obvious alteration. Let the child say what has been removed or what is different. Gradually increase the number of objects, at the same time making the changes less obvious.

5. Play scrabble. One can also use scrabble letters separately to make words, without playing the game.

6. Play any card games where the child has to remember numbers, pictures or figures. Lotto for example.

7. Practise remembering telephone numbers shown. This can also be used with auditory short-term memory problems if the numbers are read to them.

8. Practise remembering the order of letters and numbers of car numberplates while out driving. To motivate them they can get a reward for a certain number of correct ones.

9. Make a hand tachistoscope; a quick exposure device consisting of a cardboard cover, an opening, a shutter and a series of words on strips of cardboard.

10. Syllable work. Breaking up words into syllables helps reinforce the sequence of syllables in a word and is useful in helping with spelling.

11. Let the child trace a word or copy it from an example. Do not remove the example. If the child makes a mistake he has to identify and correct his own errors by looking at the example.

12. Expose a collection of objects. Cover and remove one of the objects. Show the collection again, asking the child to identify the missing object.

13. Expose a geometrical design, sequence of letters or numbers. Have the child reproduce the design, letters or numbers on paper.

14. Use white magnetic letters on a black background. This provides an eye-catching contrast for the student who is not in the habit of attending to the detail involved in the letters.

III. MOTOR PROBLEMS

Gross Motor Coordination
Children who have gross motor coordination problems appear clumsy, uncoordinated and awkward. They are often unable to compete with their age mates in athletics activities. They may collide frequently with tables, chairs and other equipment in their classrooms. Problems in this area are often accompanied with self-concept problems and feelings of inadequacy. Gross motor activities involve all the muscles of the body and the ability to move various parts of the body on command, controlling body movements in relation to various outer and inner elements such as gravity, laterality and body midlines. The purpose of these activi-

ties is to develop smoother, more effective body movements, and also to add to the child's sense of spatial orientation and body consciousness. The child with this problem needs an individual program of physical exercises. Initially, he does not benefit much from group games or group exercises. The remedial teacher must provide individual help for every problem the child experiences.

REMEDIAL PROCEDURES

1. The child must take part in locomotor activities, like walking backwards, forwards and sideways. The child walks through a straight or curved path marked on the floor to a target goal. The path may be wide or narrow, but the narrower the path the more difficult the task. Variations of this course may be done with the child walking with arms in different positions, carrying objects, dropping objects along the way, such as balls into containers, or with eyes focused on various parts of the room.

2. The child can do animal walks. Have him imitate the walks of various animals. Elephant walk: bent forward at the waist allowing the arms to hang down and taking big steps while swinging from side to side. Rabbit hop: place hands on the floor, do deep knee bends and move feet together between hands. Crab walk: crawl forwards and backwards, face up. Duck walk: walk with hands on knees while doing a deep knee bend. Worm walk: with hands and feet on the floor take small steps first with the feet then with the hands.

3. Moon walk. The child can imitate the leaping kangaroo steps of the astronauts on the moon.

4. Stepping stones. You can place objects on the floor for stepping stones, indicating the placement for right foot and left foot by colour, or the letter "r" and "l". The child is to follow the course by placing the correct foot on each stepping stone.

5. Box game. The child has two boxes the size of shoe boxes, one behind and one in front. The child steps into the front box with both feet, moves the rear box from behind to the front and then steps into that. The child can use different hands to move boxes and use alternating feet. They must move towards the finish line.

6. Ladder walk. Place a ladder flat on the ground. Have the child walk between rungs forwards, backwards and hopping.

7. Angels in the snow. Have the child lie down with his back on the floor and move limbs on command. Begin with bilateral commands, eg move feet apart as far as possible, move arms along the ground until they meet above the head. Follow with unilateral commands, eg move left arm only, move left leg only, and finally give cross-lateral commands, eg move left arm and right leg.

8. Obstacle crawl. Create an obstacle course with boxes, hoops, table barrels, chairs and so on, and have the child cover a predetermined course, going through, under, over and around various objects.

9. The skateboard provides another technique for gross body motor activities. This can be done lying on the stomach, kneeling or standing, and the surface can be flat or a downhill slope.

10. Jumping jacks. Jump, putting the feet wide apart while clapping hands above the head. Variations of this can be made by asking the child to make quarter turns, half turns and full turns, or by asking the child to jump to the left, right, north or south.

11. Hopping. Hop on one foot at a time. Alternate the feet while hopping. Hop in rhythmical patterns, left, left, right, right, or left, left, right, or right, right, left.

12. Bouncing. Bouncing on a trampoline, bedsprings, mattress or a large truck tyre tube.

13. Skipping. This is a difficult activity for children with poor motor coordination. It combines rhythm, balance, body movement and coordination. Many children need help to learn to skip.

14. Hoop games. Hoops of various sizes from the hoola-hoop down, can be used to develop skills. Twist them round the arms, legs, waist, bounce balls in them, toss bean bags in them, step in and out of them.

15. Rope skills. A length of rope can be used to perform a variety of exercises. Have the child put the rope around designated parts of the body: knees, ankles, hips, to teach body image. Have the child follow directions. Put the rope around chairs, under a table, through a lampshade, jump back and forth or sideways over the rope, or make shapes, letters or numbers with the rope.

Fine Motor Coordination
Students who have fine motor coordination problems frequently have difficulty manipulating objects or performing

tasks with their fingers. These problems often appear in activities such as colouring, writing, lacing shoes, buttoning clothes, putting objects together and using scissors. The result of these students' efforts to use fine motor skills will often look like those of a much younger student. Although some children may do well at gross motor activities their fine motor abilities performance may be poor.

REMEDIAL PROCEDURES

1. Tracing. Trace lines, pictures, designs, letters or numbers on tracing paper, plastic or stencils. Use directional arrows, colour cues and numbers to help the child.

2. Water control. Carry and pour water into measured buckets from pitchers to specified levels. Use smaller amounts and finer measurements to make the task more difficult. The use of coloured water makes it more interesting.

3. Cutting with scissors. Have children cut with scissors, choosing activities that are appropriate to their needs. Cut out marked geometric shapes such as squares, rectangles and triangles. Draw a different coloured line to indicate a change of direction in cutting.

4. Lacing. A piece of cardboard punched with holes, or a pegboard, can be used for this activity. A design or picture is made on the board and the child follows the pattern by weaving or sewing through the holes with a heavy shoelace, wool or similar cord.

5. Stacking blocks and fitting objects together.

6. Pencil and paper activities. Colouring books, readiness

books, dot to dot books and kindergarten books frequently provide good paper and pencil activities for fine motor and eye/hand development.

7. Clipping clothes pegs. Clothes pegs can be clipped onto a line or a box. Children can be timed by counting the number of clothes pegs clipped in a specified time.

8. Copying designs. Children can look at a geometric design and copy it onto a piece of paper.

9. Paper folding. Some paper folding activities are useful for the development of eye/hand coordination, following directions and fine motor control.

10. Playing marbles, chequers, tic-tac-toe and jacks. The game of jacks provides opportunities for development of eye/hand coordination, rhythmical movements and fine finger and hand movements.

11. Any work with pieces of clay or play dough helps to strengthen the finger muscles. Get the child to make various forms, animals and objects, with finer and finer detail.

12. Children can string beads or macaroni onto a thread.

13. For an older girl, sewing can be a useful exercise. She can draw patterns onto a piece of material and she can try and follow those using a needle and thread.

14. Snapping press studs or buttoning buttons, tying shoes, doing up zips; all of these can be useful in developing fine motor coordination.

15. Circles. The child can practise making large circles on a board, or piece of paper, with one hand and with two hands clockwise and counter-clockwise.

Body Image
Body image refers to a person's awareness of his or her body and its capabilities. Body image activities are designed to help the child develop accurate images of the location of parts of the body and the function of these parts.

REMEDIAL PROCEDURES
1. Point to body parts. Ask the child to point to the various parts of the body: nose, right elbow, left ankle and so on. This activity is more difficult with the eyes closed. Children can also lie down on the floor and be asked to touch various parts of their bodies. This activity is more difficult if done in a rhythmic pattern. Use a metronome, for example.

2. Make a life-sized tracing of a classmate's body and then of their own body.

3. Have students draw in the face, fingernails and other details on a sheet of paper with an outline of their body.

4. Have students crawl under, over and through an obstacle course. Ask them describe what they are doing while moving through the course.

5. Have students practise moving and touching various parts of their own bodies while facing a full length mirror.

6. Cut pictures of the body into two pieces and then into several pieces and have students reassemble them into the whole.

7. Give students partially completed drawings and ask them to draw in the missing parts.

8. A robot made from cardboard, held together at the joints with fasteners, can be moved into various positions. The children can move the limbs of the robot on command and match the positions with their own body movements.

9. Simon says. This game can be played with the eyes open and the eyes closed.

10. Puzzles. Puzzles of people, objects, animals and so forth, can be cut to show functional parts of the body.

11. Pantomime. The children pantomine actions that are characteristic of a certain occupation, such as a bus driver driving a bus, a police officer directing traffic, a postman delivering a letter or a chef cooking.

IV. SPATIAL PROBLEMS

The ability to determine the correct position of objects in space is of major importance for success in learning. The children with a problem in this respect have difficulties with reading, spelling and mathematics. This perceptual skill consists of the ability to locate forms that are reversed, inverted or rotated, to recognise likenesses and differences in forms and to discriminate the position of figures, letters and objects in space. The child that is unable to determine the relationship of objects to his own body often shows "b", "d", or "p" reversal, writes "sa" for "as", and 42 for 24.

REMEDIAL PROCEDURES
1. Identify geometric figures, letters or numerals on a page

containing a variety of inverted, reversed and rotated symbols.

2. Locate the direction of objects from oneself.

3. Practise physical exercises and movement experiences that develop an awareness of body parts.

4. Locate objects from verbal or written directions.

5. Imitate body positions.

6. Read maps and blueprints.

7. Arrange objects according to specific instructions, eg put the ball under the chair, put the rubber in the top drawer, put the rubber in the second drawer from the bottom.

V. PROBLEMS REGARDING RIGHT/LEFT ORIENTATION

The child with problems regarding right/left orientation has difficulty differentiating between the right and left sides of his own body. The concept of right and left on pictures or other objects also presents problems. As with previous remedial procedures the remedial program has to include multi-sensory motor activities. Programs used for the remediation of problems regarding spatial relations, gross motor coordination, body image and position in space, can also be employed for this problem, with special emphasis on right, left or right side or left side. The child will benefit from colouring or drawing certain objects such as the following: the cat to the left of the tree, the dog to the right of the house, the shoe on the doll's left foot.

Other activities that will help with discriminating between right and left are:

1. Put nail polish on the little finger of the student's left hand. Teach them that reading and writing both start at the far left-hand side.

2. Make a green tick, mark or dot on the left side of the paper where the student should start.

3. Place hands on paper and then label them as left or right. Ask the student to sort tracings of left and right hands into separate piles.

4. Have students identify left and right parts of their bodies, the bodies of others and bodies of people in pictures, eg left ear and right foot.

5. Organise a series of pictures in a left to right sequence so that they tell a story.

6. Play games that emphasise movement of the left and right sides of the body.

VI. HYPERACTIVITY

This is usually characterised by excessive movements and motor activity. The child seems to be in constant motion, tapping feet or pencils, shifting paper etc. Some suggestions for classroom management:

1. Structure lessons in the classroom so that the source of stimuli is limited and the work area is free from distraction.

2. Structure each lesson so the student can master the material within a time period that is compatible with his attention span.

3. Ask students to perform tasks and errands that permit them to move around the classroom and school building. These opportunities can be saved for the times when the student needs a break, or a change of pace.

4. Prepare a number of low-pressure fun activities for when the students need to spend a few minutes regaining control or relaxing.

5. Reinforce appropriate behaviour with free time or time to participate in preferred activities.

VII. DISTRACTION AND SHORT ATTENTION SPAN

Many students who have learning problems are easily distracted. Their attention may be led away from the assigned task by any noise, motion, light or colour in the classroom. They may pay attention to everything going on in the classroom other than the assigned task. Often, they will work on the task for a brief period of time, but not long enough to complete it. Many hyperactive students have short attention spans and are highly distractible. Procedures that are often effective when used with these students include the following:

1. Remove background noises, bulletin boards, displays and other sources of potentially distracting visual and auditory stimuli.

2. Remove all materials that are not required for completing the assignment or lesson from the student's desktop.

3. Provide the students with a specific time for completing each assigned task.

4. Place head sets on students without plugging them into a sound source in order to reduce the reception of distracting sounds.

5. Use a card with a window cut in it, or a frame, to focus the student's attention on a specific area, problem, line of print or paragraph.

6. Use a coloured placemat as the background for an assigned task. Use the student's favourite colour to restrict his or her tendency to be distracted by other visual stimuli.

7. Organise the various events of the day so that activities that tend to stimulate or excite students come after, rather than before, activities that require extended periods of concentration.

8. Seat these students so that they are facing a wall, with their backs to the other students.

9. Provide a study booth made out of a large, well-ventilated and well-lighted box that has been carpeted on the inside for comfort. Permit students to retreat to this quiet box to get away from distracting auditory and visual stimuli. DO NOT, however, use the same box as a place for punishment. On a smaller scale, sections of cardboard can be fastened together as a barrier to isolate them when they are unable to handle the level of visual stimuli around them.

INDEX